Polio, Marco.
The hole

The Hole

Marco Polio

Sugar Loaf Press

ISBN 0-9700702-5-X
Library of Congress Control Number: 00-131486

10 9 8 7 6 5 4 3 2 1

Sugar Loaf Press
PO Box 375
Granville, Oh 43023

Printed in the USA

This book is dedicated to Americans past, present, and future, who struggle against the wheel.

I

A streak. Then another—over hydrants, around signs, up
the long, pitted cement sidewalk that lines Front Street,
across the humped bridge and above the railroad tracks,
toward Goodwill Park; I find more pleasure watching these
runners lugging themselves around the city, capricious,
thunderous, as if the city could take it. There are no hanging plants in our fair town, these giraffes are all I have.

"You heard about old man Selowt?" huffing, puffing
runner number one wheezes to runner number two, his big
fect slapping the pavement.

"I heard he was in bad shape."

"Bad shape? He's toast."

"You're kidding. What happened?" runner two breathes,
barely able to form a question.

"Had an aneurysm the other night. He's in a coma."

"Oh, man."

"Yeah."

"What's the prognosis?"

Runner one shakes his head beaded with newborn drops, a misted morning orchid. "I don't think he's going to come out of it. Luckily, there's the boy."

"The boy?"

"His nephew. He's got power of attorney. The land hasn't been signed over yet, you know."

"Yeah, I've been reading. . ."

"The nephew, he's a big Bovines fan."

"That's good."

"No kidding."

"He going to sell?"

"Why wouldn't he?"

"I don't know."

"I mean, that land's going to buy him a lot of pencils."

"But he doesn't *have* to sell."

"He's a poet, of sorts. They don't really know much about him."

"Nobody can *force* him to sell, can they?"

"Why wouldn't he? Most poets are broke."

"But *he's* not getting the money. . . is he?"

"Why wouldn't he be getting it? If he can sign over the land, he can get the money."

"Poets are a funny type."

"You bet they are."

"Eccentrics."

"Quacks, if truth be told."

"Aw, who knows what he's going to do," runner two says absently. The pain in his side allowed only cursory attention to anything else. "Come on. Let's stop for a soda."

The poet, the quack, it had a name. One Jerry Wrigdd. In the months since Selowt's aneurysm, Wrigdd had been dogged by the press, harassed by just about everybody who recognized him, had his car burned, and was hung in effigy by somebody working at the Freedom National Bank; yet he remained a shadow.

Seldom seen in daylight, he strolled the old neighborhood after dark, often past midnight, with no apparent destination. Average in height and build, young, about thirty-five, he wore an old wool coat, its lining pulling out in jagged strands. The coat had three different kinds of buttons, and dull, gray spots from where a cat used to curl in it each night. It was an old coat, not just any coat, the one *she* used to wear when it was bitter cold and he would use the flimsy brown jacket instead, so she could be warm and look nice with her long tumbling curls and magical green eyes and wide pink smile. His hands moved a little. They lay dead deep in his pockets. He wore a Bovines cap pulled down to his eyebrows and past his ears; not a very nice hat, mottled with grease and dirt, tattered, the only one he owned since he was a teen. He shuffled his feet in the snow that wasn't plowed, and kicked at the edge of the snow that was. Sometimes he sat on benches in the park well into the night, motionless, silent.

Some said he was simple. Others that he wasn't simple, but depressed. Still others that he wasn't simple, or depressed, but just someone who never had much attention as a child. Some nights he stopped in at the old bar in the neighborhood, and for the most part was left alone. He used to come in with her. They'd sit at one of the small rickety tables and drink and laugh and act like a sailor and his date, he exploring with his hands, and she giggling and enjoying the attention from all the leering, envious professionals in their ties and hard shoes. They often drank too much and paid for it the next day, but in those days paying for it meant sleeping it off in bed together, or slumped like rags on the floor one on top of the other, and that wasn't half bad either. Now when he came in he was given the corner booth near the kitchen, even when the bar was empty, and he sat with cold stillness staring into his pint glass. He'd swirl the glass to watch the beads of carbon dioxide move like clouds and rise to form a new head, and you figured he was probably thinking of her then, but maybe he wasn't. Maybe he just did it out of curiosity or boredom. The girls were nice to him. He smiled with small effort at them, without moving his head, as they passed in and out through the swinging kitchen door. They brought him new pints when he needed it. They were quiet and unobtrusive around him and gossiped only after turning the corner.

II

Jerry Wrigdd. A dark coat, shuffling feet, the city of Cowopolis now his hostage. Not for what he had done, but for what he refused to do. The most mindless of tasks, a fleeting ripple in time measured to the right of decimal points. A gush of a lilac breeze, or beep of a car, or sudden clap of thunder: the signing of one's signature on a piece of paper.

For five months now his refusal had created, shall I say, a slight disturbance. The old stadium, built twenty-five years ago and in its time hailed as a modern day eighth wonder, had already been sold. The developer who bought it wasted no time in demolition. The Bovines were to lease the nearby university stadium, but that lease was for two years only. University officials made it clear that the lease would not be extended under any circumstances. Without the new stadium, the Bovines were a team without a home.

Enter principal owner and Bovine president, Theo Usurper. Usurper, the son of an immigrant, had presided over the team for nearly thirty years. Infamous to many, at the tender age of thirty-eight he fired the man many considered to be the most brilliant football mind of his era, Paul Black. Big on brash, short on savvy and often cash, Usurper managed over the next three decades to tempt, tease, and entice his followers into believing he had the Bovines marching in the right direction, across the vast desert of mediocrity, just on the cusp of the next championship. Salvation was just around the corner. So Theo Usurper, the son of an immigrant, swore.

The sticky-fingered Usurper got his hands into many business ventures, most of which he had no business being in. He lost a great deal of money. There had been a special levy in the last election, Issue 1. A vote for Issue 1 meant that Usurper would have his new stadium, financed mostly by the county, plus a 50% revenue share of concessions. He hadn't had that at the old stadium. If the city voted "no", then he would pack up and take the Bovines elsewhere. To Denver, or Boston, or St. Louis. Each city had recently been abandoned by its own team and was hungry for another. Denver in particular had already passed a new stadium levy. The city promised unprecedented tax abatement, a 50/50 joint ownership, and an even better 60% revenue share of concessions. Usurper, so he declared, wanted to keep the Bovines in Cowopolis. His hands, so he swore, were tied. A "no" vote would force him to move his beloved Bovines, and that, he said, would break his heart.

The city responded, out of fear, or conditioning, it's hard

to say. The vote, the "yes" vote, was overwhelming. It was hailed as a victory for the city's children, a genuine historic moment, a turning point. All seemed well in Cowopolis, and then *he* entered the picture.

Another rally was held; Cowopolis, you stubborn boy. They turned out in numbers like nothing this city has ever seen, carrying signs, dressed in black and white cow hides, wearing Bovine hats, Bovine udders, Bovine scarves, chanting Bovine chants, beating innocent mailboxes and innocent hoods of cars, stopping traffic, shaking fists, the name *Wrigdd* foaming from their mouths. Men, women, grandpas and grandmas; babes-in-arms, foundry men, carpenters, bankers, barbers, billboard makers; secretaries, waitresses, office managers, drunks and teetotalers, priests and rabbis, leftists and rightists—why even democrats and republicans walking arm-in-arm, side-by-side, caught on film for all of posterity. I can tell you, it was a mobilization!

Man on the street, you black and white spotted beast, snarling, huffing and puffing and baring your teeth—speak, speak, I say! I want to feel your lava spewing forth.

"Mmmooooo!"

"Mmmooooo!"

"Mmmooooo!"

"Mmmmmmooooooo!"

"Rrrrrooooooo!"

"Mmmmmmooooooo!"

Mmmooooove it, brother. Here come the sisters, the Bovine Belles, bobbie sox and pigtails, perfumed and pom-pommed (in perfect harmony no less).

"Save the cows, save the beef, save our city, save the team! Mmmooooo!

"Save the cows, save the beef, save the stadium, no more grief! Mmmooooo!

"Save the cows, save the beef, save our city, kill the thief! Mmmuuuuurder the bum!

"Save the cows, save the beef, save our city, save the team! Bovines! Bovines! Rah—rah—rah!"

Mmmaaaaarvelous, girls—

"Save the cows, save the beef, sign the paper, you crummy little piece of—"

Thank you, thank you, thank you, girls. Move along now. Lovely costumes. Oh yes, terrific haunches, pert udders you have there. Beautiful hooves. Thank you, girls.

Mmmaaaaake way! The future approaches in over-sized, authentic jerseys, caps, sweatshirts and cleats; the youth of Cowopolis, mad as a mule stampede. What say you, boys? What would you like to see come from this civil demonstration?

"Basically, we just want the Bovines to stay," says one nine-year-old sponge.

"Yeah," says his echo, "we want the Bovines to stay."

"Jerry Wrigdd is a jerk."

"Yeah, Jerry Wrigdd is a jerk."

"It's not even his land, it's his uncle's."

"Yeah, his uncle's."

"If his poor uncle wasn't in a coma, he'd sign the paper."

"Yeah. He would."

"Why doesn't he just sign it? Everybody thinks he's a jerk for not signing it."

"Yeah, the biggest jerk in the world."

"If I was the mayor, I'd make him sign it."

"Me too."

"And if he didn't sign it, I'd blow his brains out."

"Pow! Bang!"

"Just like the Demonic Destroyer!"

"Zap! Rat-tat-tat-tat!"

"Body slam him to the ground."

"Whomp!"

I see. Hmm. So. Anything more to add?

"Texas Executioners," the boy says, pulls out a powder blue cap from his back pocket, and plants it on his head.

The Texas Executioners?

"Made it to the Big Bowl last year. They kick ass!"

And you?

"Boston Minutemen," says the echo. From beneath his over-sized, authentic Bovines jersey he pulls out an over-sized, authentic Minutemen jersey and stretches it wide below his jack-o-lantern smile. "They *won* the Big Bowl last year!"

Meaning?

The boy looks up, as though he had been asked to put on a dress. He replies, a monosyllabic grunt, the gist of which, I think, was *duuuuh!*

There comes a cloud. No, more like a hurricane. Manicured faces and blinding smiles. Camera flashes and scurrying feet. At the epicenter, the mayor. Queen termite. Electro-magnet.

Oh, mayor! Mmmaaaaayor!

"Hmm? Who's that?"

Why, mayor—

"Why? Why?" he brightens like a new bulb. "Why *what*?"

No, it's not a question—

"Of course, a question, that's why I'm here—out with it, man, haven't got all day you know."

Well, all right; Mr. Mayor, my question concerns—

"Question? Whoa, sorry fella, no time for questions. I'm due to speak momentarily," he squeaks in a panic, and the hurricane continues on its meandering course toward city hall.

The rally began shortly before sundown. The chairman of the Save The Bovines Brigade stepped onto the pedestal of Herbert Horatio Steele's statue; Indian slayer, part-time minister, and founder of Cowopolis. He used the granite nose of Herbert Horatio's dog, Sniffer, as a seat.

The chairman talked of traditional American ideals, now being put to the test: honor, pride, courage, resolve. Of doing the right thing.

"These ideals," he said, "are what built Cowopolis into the thriving community it is today, from the dirty, dusty prairie it once was. These ideals were the bricks that formed the foundation of our blue collar, workingman's football team. An organization steeped in history, tradition, greatness. The Bovines represent not only all that is good about our great country, but the effort and commitment it takes to achieve such greatness."

The crowd roared. There were whistles and gongs and fight songs from fifty years ago. They stomped booted feet and clapped mittened hands. Eyes frosted over from nostalgia and heartache.

"The enemy," cried the chairman, "is out *there*."

"Usurper!" some shouted.

"No!" he shouted back. "No, not *him*! Usurper is only doing what any man might do in his shoes."

The crowd grumbled.

"That's right! Hear me out. Usurper has been the owner of this team for thirty odd years, and in those thirty years he's given us some great teams. He's poured his money— millions—into the Bovines. He's operated in the old stadium without complaint, while other owners have been given new ones by their cities. He's asked nothing of you, his loyal supporters, but support itself. And now when situations beyond his control have forced his hand, you cry foul. I say no! No! Usurper is red, white and blue—through and through. Just like our great founder, Herbert Horatio Steele, just like all of *you*.

"The real evil in this whole rotten mess is that coward, that gutless, unemployed, good-for-nothing traitor. You know who I mean. *He's* the one you should be directing your anger at. He's the one who seized an opportunity,

11

from a poor helpless invalid no less, a blood relative, and pulled the rug right out from under us. He's the enemy. The poet, Jerry Wrigdd!

"For months, from the day his good uncle was struck down, Wrigdd has held this city by the throat. Time and time again Mr. Usurper, our mayor, myself and others have tried to work with him. Tried reasoning with him. Tried to understand his point of view, so that all parties—not just Usurper, or the Bovines, but Wrigdd as well, yes—come out of this thing ahead. But all we've gotten is silence. He doesn't want to speak to us, he doesn't want to explain his position. He says he'll meet Usurper in Goodwill Park, then doesn't show. He says he understands our predicament, says he feels regret, but offers us nothing tangible. I say to you, citizens of Cowopolis, one man and one man only is to blame for the current situation. One man, acting out of a self-motivated greed. One man who has taken the key to the city and has hidden it beneath his pillow. That one man is Jerry Wrigdd."

III

"Miss Green?"

Beauty that you are, melter of men's broad and ashen faces, catapult to goodness, lover of living things. She, with gloves and Wellingtons. She, sun-freckled nose and apron pulled snug. She, rare oasis in the expanding desert.

The two men stepped into the greenhouse, which was warm and humid and smelled of baking dirt. They introduced themselves as friends of Theo Usurper, and were skeptical when she asked who he was.

"Who is Theo Usurper?" the tall one, Dickson, said. He removed his gloves, balled them up, and stuffed them into the pockets of his overcoat.

Miss Green, sitting on a stool beside the potting bench, wrinkled her nose at the sun and looked up at him. "Is he someone I should know?" she asked.

"Miss Green," Dickson said, "we were wondering, we

were hoping you could give us some information."

"What kind of information?"

"It's about a friend of yours," Dickson said

"I told you, I don't know any Theo Usurper."

"Tell me, do you know a man by the name of Jerry Wrigdd?"

"Jerry?" Mary Green said with a start. She had not heard his name for many months.

"You knew him, didn't you?"

She fell silent, lost in remembering. "Yes," she said then. "I knew him."

"Can you tell us about him?"

"What do you want to know?"

"Anything you can give us," Dickson said.

"He's not in trouble, is he?" she said looking up, her eyes passing between them. "I mean besides being harassed by everyone."

"Well, no, not really."

"Is he?" she said, taking hold of his arm.

"Miss Green."

"Oh," she said then, the light turning on.

"Miss Green."

"It's *you*."

"Miss Green."

"I didn't recognize his name. I know who you are."

"Miss Green, please."

"Theo Usurper. The great Theo Usurper."

"Can you tell us anything? We won't be but a minute."

"Shepherd of lemmings."

"Anything?"

"King of the temper tantrum."

"We'd appreciate your cooperation."

"Extortionist extraordinaire."

"Ho, jeez. You're not making it easy on me, Miss."

"I don't think I can help you," she said, folding her arms.

"You don't?" Dickson said anxiously.

"You heard me right."

"And why's that?" he said with a hopeful grin, leaning forward.

"Because," she said. "The things I could tell you about him you wouldn't understand. And the things you want to get from me I know nothing about."

"Don't be so sure about that, Miss. We'd be glad to hear anything you'd like to tell us."

"You can't travel through time. You have only two eyes. Your heart ends with your own personal fences. You couldn't possibly understand him."

The other one chuckled.

"Knock it off," Dickson told him. "I see."

"No, you don't. You don't see at all."

"Well, you got me there, 'cause you haven't told me anything," he said, lifting his hands in his pockets. He waited, looking at her patiently. He took out a small pad, his teeth delicately nibbled at the inside of his mouth.

"Jerry Wrigdd was a locksmith," she said.

"A locksmith."

"That's right. You know what a locksmith is?"

"Yeah, I know what a locksmith is. He was a locksmith."

"If you want to know."

"Ma'am, I don't think that's right."

"Not on your little pad there?"

"Uh, no, it isn't."

"So are you going to write it down, or am I wasting my breath?"

"I'll remember. A locksmith."

"He could pick any lock ever made. Do you believe me?"

"I don't know," Dickson said. "I don't think so."

"Would you believe me if I said he had the longest arms in the world—they could reach across oceans to the oppressed, disadvantaged, the blind. Would you believe me?"

"Um, well now, I don't know. I don't think so. I think maybe you got a little stash of homegrown hidden in one of those tins," he said chuckling to himself, turning stiffly to grin at his friend.

"You think it's pretty funny."

"No, not really."

"I think *you're* pretty funny."

"Hey, whatever," Dickson said, lifting his hands. "I'm here to please."

"You're not writing in the pad."

"I got a good memory. Anyhow, that's what Tweedle-Dee is for."

"You really want to know what he's like?" she said, eyeing them each carefully.

"If you don't mind."

"You'd hate him."

"Ma'am, everybody hates him."

16

"That's right, they do, don't they. Well. You'd hate him even if he gave you your stadium. You'd hate him if you met him in a bar. You'd hate him if you bumped into him on the street. You'd hate him because you see, he's not like anybody else. You'd think he was just noise."

"Oh," Dickson said. "One of them kind."

"That's right, one of them kind."

"You're right. Probably would hate the guy."

"Nobody likes noise, do they? Everybody wants music. Soft, soothing music to carry them away. Isn't that right?"

"What do you expect?"

"I don't expect anything anymore."

"Expect little and everything's gravy," Dickson said happily. "That's what I say. Lower your expectations and the world's nothing but gravy."

"You see, he wouldn't do that."

"Well, some guys never learn."

"And some guys don't give in."

"The world breaks them and then they wonder why."

"The world could never break him," she said, "even in his loneliness. Tell me, Usurper's mouse, do you have any idea what it's like to be lonely?"

"Lonely? Sure. Everybody gets lonely. When I get lonely me and Cheeks here, we take our rubber teeth and hit the bars. Funny how you can meet anybody with a pair of them goofy rubber teeth. Girls just go crazy laughing."

"And before the rubber teeth?"

"Before the rubber teeth," Dickson said, thumping his head. "Oh jeez, I don't know. Had them rubber teeth for a long time. Can't remember offhand. Drank more beer, I

17

guess."

"What if you had no rubber teeth, no beer, no Cheeks to go out with; what if you had your loneliness, and ten thousand others as real as your own?"

"Imagine I'd be a real drag."

"I imagine so."

"Like your friend."

"To you, maybe. To me, he was anything but. He had a gift. He would give you what you really needed, and most of the time you had no idea what that was. Ah. But there's no point in trying to give anything to a world of geniuses swimming in a sea of gravy, is there?"

"So that's your locksmith."

"No," she said. "That was my savior."

"She's nutty, boss," Cheeks said. "Come on."

"Knock it off," Dickson told him.

"But she's nutty."

"I said clam up. Hey," he said, touching her arm, "what do you mean?"

"It's right before your eyes, Usurper's mouse. It's always been right before your eyes," she said.

"What the hell are you talking about?"

"Yes," she said. "What the hell am I talking about?"

IV

Of his guilt, there was no question. But of what crime? Nothing had yet happened. Precisely the point, as most Cowopolitans would tell you; but how can you charge a man for *not* doing something? Look, some said, a man can be considered good without proof or reason. It's self-evident. It's understood, accepted on the whole rather than deconstructed on the part. So why must a bad man, an evil man, be granted the loophole of proof? Isn't evil just as self-evident, as easily understood? Why was this man able to move about freely? Free to roam the shadows at night, free to remain silent; is there no justice? The citizens of Cowopolis wanted to know.

"You trying to piss me off or something?" Usurper grumbled, looking over his black-rimmed trifocals. "'Cause if you are, you're doing a hell of a job."

"No, boss, I'm not trying to piss you off," Dickson said.

"Shut up."

"Okay."

"What did she say?"

"I, um, forgot."

"You got emphysema or something?"

"No, boss."

"I can hear you breathing all the way over here. What the hell's the matter with you?"

"I don't know, boss."

"Well, keep your breathing down, I'm trying to think. So. What'd you find out?"

"Well, let's see now," Dickson said, eyes looking up to the ceiling.

"I'm warning you," Usurper said, cocking his finger.

"Okay. Right. You know, he's some kind of screwball, just like you thought."

"Cheeks said something about him being a locksmith with long arms."

"That's right."

"Like a safe cracker. Is that what you're telling me?"

"Uh, yeah. Well, no."

"Shut up."

"Okay."

"What else?"

"Uh, well, Miss Green, the young lady, you could say she thought an awful lot of that Wrigdd guy. I'm not sure, but I think she was speaking metaphorically."

"Meta-*what*?"

"Metaphorically."

"You making fun of me?"

"No, boss."

"You smell like puke. What the hell's the matter with you; don't you know what a shower is?"

"Sure, boss. I shower up nice most every day."

"Shut up."

"Okay."

"What else?"

"What else, let's see. Nothing else, really. Said he was a lonely guy type. She asked me if I ever been lonely and I told her why sure, I've been lonely, everybody's been lonely sometimes. That's what certain magazines and the Internet are for. I don't think your man is into those things though. He—"

"You finished?"

"I'm finished, boss," Dickson said, putting his hands in his pockets.

Usurper shook his head.

"Where'd you go after seeing the girl?"

"We came right over, boss."

"Shut up. Where?"

"The Raw Oyster."

"In the middle of the afternoon, you go to The Raw Oyster?"

"Drinks are half-price from three to five."

Usurper jumped to his feet, but as the in-box left his hand Dickson was already fast out the door.

A few minutes later, mayor Mayeye and police chief Hyantite knocked and came in. They had come at Usurper's request.

"Come on in," Usurper offered, "sit, sit." He moved to

the corner of his desk and sat there, ruminating for some time. "Gentlemen," he finally said, folding his arms. "So where do we stand?"

"Same as before," the mayor said, his face like a gray flat tire in the meaty palm of his hand. "There's nothing. The guy's got nothing on him whatsoever. I don't know what to tell you."

"We could bring him in for, say, a minor drug possession," chief Hyantite said. "We could plant it easy enough. But everybody knows he's clean. It'd smell of a set-up from the start. The press gets hold of it, and—"

"Which they will," Mayeye said, lifting his lips to speak.

"They will," Hyantite agreed. "There's some major exposure there."

"We've got some major exposure already," Usurper broke in. "This city, gentlemen, is about to be euthanized."

"I know, I realize that, Theo," a frustrated Hyantite said. "But we can only do so much. We can't bring him in on nothing. And we sure as hell can't hold him on it."

"We can if there's no other way," Usurper pressed. "We have to."

"It won't fly," Hyantite shook his head. "We're going to be crucified, all three of us."

"Correction. *He's* going to be crucified."

"We gotta keep our wits about us," the mayor muttered to himself, "step back, look at it from all angles. That's it. Take our time. Things will work out."

"Mayor, things work out because somebody makes them work out. That somebody is us." Usurper got up and began pacing the room. "Look, you've got your polls to worry about mayor, and chief, you've got the riots to contend with. I've got a professional football team to run. Do you understand me? Do you know what I'm saying? Half a billion dollars, gentlemen. That's where *I'm* coming from." He stopped by the window. He stared out without seeing anything, imagining instead his new stadium gleaming beneath an autumn sky. "Now there's a fine piece of property right over there with a line of bulldozers waiting to get started. That's my property. Me and Selowt had an agreement; by rights it's mine. *Mine*, do you understand? I'm not about to let some flaky poet turn out the lights. That's not going to happen, see? I'll tell you what *is* going to happen. You two are going to find something to bring him in on. You're going to do it, and you're going to do it soon. Soon like by tomorrow, understand?"

"Theo," the mayor protested, lifting his whole flat head from his hand.

"That's how it's going to be," Usurper insisted. "It can be done. It will be done. That punk's a criminal; it's time you started treating him like one."

Jerry Wrigdd was arrested in his apartment the next day, brought down to police headquarters, and charged with disturbing the peace and inciting a riot. Mayeye made the call to Usurper himself, who ran the two blocks over. You'd have thought they just bagged a man-eating tiger. Handshakes went round like kisses on New Year's Eve.

"Who got him?" Usurper wanted to know.

"Here's the man," came an answer, and a tall, slim officer was pushed forward.

"You get him?" Usurper said to the officer.

"Yes, sir."

"Brilliant. What's your name?"

"Miller, sir."

"Miller, you, my friend, are a hero. And I want to be the first one to shake your hand."

For the first time since the end of the Vietnam War the Cowopolis Daily Press ran an extra, with officer Miller and Theo Usurper beaming like a couple of Christmas brides on the front page.

"Ladies and gentlemen," the mayor nudged forward, speaking to the cameras, "I present officer Miller. A real Elliot Ness, ferreting out the weasel we've all been looking for. Miller," Mayeye declared, looking up at the tall officer, patting him on the back, "you have just apprehended the most notorious scoundrel this city—perhaps the entire state—has ever had the misfortune to encounter. Thanks to your swift action, your heady tenacity, your sheer bravery, Cowopolis might once again return to happier times."

"Nothing to it," Miller said.

"The modesty."

"No, really. It was a piece of cake."

"A bashful white night, ladies and gentlemen!"

"Routine."

"Miller," whispered the mayor from the side of his mouth.

"Came without a peep. Actually, he's quite a nice fellow—"

"Thank you, officer Miller," the mayor said, nudging the man back into the obscurity of life behind the cameras. All attention now focused on Mayeye, Usurper, and chief Hyantite as they went over the apprehension once again, gave conjecture as to what this might mean to the stadium, and answered questions concerning any sort of pardon Wrigdd might be given once he relented and sold the property.

Outside, officer Miller pulled his cap firmly on his head. He began walking down the steps when he stopped and turned back to look at headquarters. Something bugged him. It wasn't all the attention, nor residual nervousness from being on television. It was *him*. There was something about that man he couldn't put a finger on, but it gnawed at him just the same. He hadn't said much while sitting in the back of the squad car. Mostly he just stared out the window.

Miller shrugged his shoulders and continued on down the steps. For the rest of the day he was in a daze. He wanted to go back and sit down with Wrigdd and have a talk, but he couldn't do that. It wasn't his place as a simple police officer. That night he had the most beautiful dreams. When he woke in the morning the dreams lingered in his mind, but when he went to tell his wife about them he could remember no details, only that they were unlike any dreams he had ever had.

V

The moment of redemption. Of revelation, exaltation,
triumph and vindication. The moment predator meets prey.
The moment of shackling and unshackling, of certainty and
more certainty, and then beyond certainty to God, and from
Him all else. To fife and drum, to fife and drum.

Usurper walked the long hallway alone, floating in
happiness, plump with supreme fulfillment. He paused
outside room 451. He wondered what he was going to find
beyond the door. Several thoughts came to him, but he
wiped his mind clean of them; he wanted his first vision of
the beast to be pure. Beautiful moments, he knew, were
best if kept virginal. He rubbed the sawtooth edge of the
key. The key he had been wanting to insert into the door of
room 451 for six months. The key once stolen, now in his
possession again. He slipped it in and turned. The door
popped open with a heavy clang.

There it was, the beast. The monkey wrench jamming the gears of tomorrow. It was alone, sitting in a wooden chair with its back to the door, wearing plain clothes, arms and hands free. They said it wasn't dangerous, but Usurper took no chances. His eyes never left the beast as he slowly moved around the table. His heart thumped as though some celestial marvel were being unfurled before him. He watched its disheveled, dark hair, its calculating hands, its suspicious lips; the beast slowly, sumptuously appeared. He watched and there beheld the blank, cowardly face of defiance. The face with no cause. The face of poison. The face of sabotage, resentment, deafness. The face of repugnance, ignorance, and chaos. Usurper pulled out the chair, sat down, and laid his arms upon the table like ready weapons.

"Well," he said.

Taking him by surprise, expecting a lengthy round of empty jabs before a hit, it spoke right up.

"Who are you?" Wrigdd said.

Usurper laughed, turning halfway round as if to say to someone, "Did you hear that? He wants to know who I am. How about that?" but no one was there. He rapped his knuckles on the table. "Who am *I*?" he said incredulously, amused.

"That's right," said Wrigdd, "who are you?"

"You must be kidding."

"Whatever," Wrigdd said, looking away.

"You don't know me?"

"I don't know you," he said.

"Maybe this will ring a bell," Usurper said, his voice

lowering, deepening. He leaned forward. "You've borrowed my lawn mower, and I want it back."

Wrigdd jerked his head. He looked at the man's face, up and down. So, he thought to himself. It's him.

"Mr. Jerry Wrigdd," Usurper said.

"In the flesh."

"Train robber of the new millennium."

"I'm your man."

"You're my man. You're my *man.* You little shit."

"Hey."

"I ought to strangle the life out of you right now, right here in this room. And if I did, do you know what would happen to me? I'd become the biggest hero this town has ever seen."

"True, but you'd get an 'F' for originality."

"Jerry Wrigdd," Usurper smiled, rubbing his hands together. "Jerry Wrigdd. The slippery snake, Jerry Wrigdd. Poet without a pulpit."

"Poet?"

"The great nothing poet."

"No, no poet," said Wrigdd, lowering his head.

"I heard different."

"Really?"

"Really."

"That's nice."

"Reliable sources too."

"Obsolete sources."

"Oh?"

"What's it to you?"

"Oh, I don't know. Just making conversation, trying to

28

get to know the man who doesn't want to be my friend."

"Well, you heard wrong."

"I don't think so," Usurper said with his big buck grin.

"You want something?"

"Why no, friend, I don't want a thing. I thought we could sit and chat the afternoon away, maybe go down to the rec hall and watch reruns of Andy Griffith, or play pool. Do you like to play pool? Cards are good too. What kind of card games do you like to play? . . . Do I *want* something?"

"You brought me in, didn't you?"

"I'll tell you what, son. You're right, I do want something."

"Let me guess."

"You don't have to guess," Usurper said, "here's the deal. I want you to sign the property over to me. Until now you've resisted. You've resisted even discussing it. I believe you've got your reasons, but I don't know what they are, you won't tell me. Well, here you are. Here I am. Guess what? Now's our chance."

Wrigdd shrugged.

"I want to know why you won't sign. I want to find out why, and then perhaps we can come to a better understanding. And then, who knows?"

"You might invite me to Christmas parties."

"Anything's possible."

"It's not that complicated," said Wrigdd without further prompting. "Okay, I'll tell you why. You see, I'm chained to something, and it won't let go. It holds me back, it slows me down. When I want to run, it makes me walk. When I want to jump, it keeps me grounded. I can't escape it. It's like a shadow, following me wherever I go, but it's big, heavy, I'm nothing against it. I don't fight it. I understand it, it frees me. I can see things, I can go places. Do you understand?" Wrigdd asked the question earnestly.

"Sounds to me like you need a heavy duty pair of snips."

"That's what I used to think. I used to hack at it day and night, until I realized it wasn't going anywhere. I stopped trying. I let go, gave myself to it. It consumed me, it grew larger, dwarfing me. Then I began to see. Then I began to move, to travel, to feel. Do you understand?"

"Surely if you can see so well, you see what's going to happen to this city because of whatever it is you just described chained to your ankles. This city will fall into the hills. All because of you."

"Cowopolis may just do that," Wrigdd agreed.

"But it doesn't have to, there's still time."

"You're asking me to feed an addict."

"I'm asking you to help your fellow man."

"It's your creation. You should be the one weaning them."

"Mine?" Usurper twisted his neck in surprise.

"Yours, theirs."

"But you do have a warped perception."

"How do you feel about that?" asked Wrigdd.

"How do I feel about what?"

"How do you feel about your contribution to the trivialization of humanity?"

"I feel frustrated because I have to deal with the likes of you," Usurper answered, looking over his trifocals.

"We all have to deal with unpleasant things."

"Some more than others," Usurper sighed. "God. You are a headache."

Wrigdd laughed. Usurper rubbed his eyes. The two men stared at each other.

"Look," Usurper said, "what's it going to take?"

"A century or two."

"Come again?"

"Nothing."

"I'm willing to work with you."

"You probably are," Wrigdd said, "but I don't see it."

"Well, try. Damn it anyway."

"You know, my teacher used to say that. But he'd slam his fist down on the table and make horrible faces, like he was going to kill me. Just thought I'd tell you that."

"Jesus Christ. You are an impudent bastard, aren't you?"

"No, just tired," Wrigdd replied.

"You know, you're in deep trouble, son."

"Oh, I know."

"I don't think you do."

"Disturbing the peace? Okay. If you say so."

"Today," Usurper nodded. "But who knows what tomorrow will bring."

"See, that's what I like about life—the unexpected."

"I mean it," Usurper warned him. "We've all had enough of you. You've had your fun. You can walk away from this thing, no problem. You can be a rich man. A celebrity. I'll be envious. But if you think you're going to push it another inch, then I can tell you you're making a big mistake. Do you understand me, Jerry?"

"I understand everything about you and that stadium."

31

"I'm not sure if you do. I'm not sure you know what it means to me."

"You're here, aren't you?"

"Yes, that's right. I'm here."

"You're a big man. Big men don't waste their time on little men who are brought in for disturbing the peace."

"Good boy."

"I wonder; does that make me a big man too?"

"You? No. You're a very small man."

"Shucks."

"But you can do a big thing."

Usurper pulled out an envelope from his jacket. He opened it, removed the documents, and laid them on the table. Mixed in with the documents was a check. The check for twenty million dollars.

"There it is," he said, leaning back. "The agreement. The check. You. Me. Our date with destiny."

"You're going to break the chair," Wrigdd said.

"Jerry, Jerry, Jerry. What's he going to do; is he going to be brave, do what's right, be hailed as the temporarily misguided hero of Cowopolis?"

"Or?"

"Or do something else."

"A dilemma."

"Not if he has good sense. I believe he has exceptionally good sense."

"Why, thank you."

"Jerry."

"Yes?"

"Sign the paper."

"Here we go."

"You can close your eyes. I'll put it under your hand and then you can honestly say you wrote down your name, but you couldn't be sure on what. You can sleep like a baby."

"Oh boy."

"Sign it and we can both go home."

Wrigdd winced and then sat on his hands.

"Twenty million dollars, Jerry. Sign it not because you've given in to anybody or anything, but because when it comes down to it you're not a stupid man. Sign it not for me, not even for you, but for the people of this city who are now as we speak on their knees, begging you, Jerry, to open up your heart."

"God, this is pitiful."

"Jerry."

"I'm listening."

"Here's the paper. Let me put this in your hand," Usurper said. He got up, leaned over, pulled Wrigdd's hand from beneath him, and inserted the pen in the hole between his thumb and forefinger. He closed the fingers around the pen. "There."

"Mr. Usurper."

"Down with the eyelids," Usurper said, and passed his hand over them.

"I appreciate your effort."

"When I tell you, fast as you can, make your mark."

"I'm sorry."

"Just a second, almost ready."

"You know I can't."

"Okay now. Go ahead."

"But you know I can't."

"Of course you can. Would you like me to whistle for you? I can sing?"

"No," Wrigdd said opening his eyes, but then Usurper closed them again

"Any time you're ready. That's it. Good boy. It's right in front of you. A scribble is all we need. Nothing fancy or even legible. However you want to do it, son."

Patient until now, Jerry Wrigdd opened his eyes. He dropped the pen and pushed the papers out from beneath him. "No," he said. "There's nothing in this world that could get you to make me sign those papers. I said no."

VI

The limousine had gone round the city twice already. It was a pale, cold day, the kind of day like so many in winter to endure and then forget. But for these men the day offered more. Inside the limousine was warmth, comfort, possibility.

On one side sat the mayor, chief of police, and Usurper. Across the small table of vibrating drinks sat a lawyer from New York and a special consultant from Washington, D.C. As the world passed steadily by outside they had, after two hours of fruitless discussion, come upon a word. This word had been uttered, immediately laughed at, ridiculed as preposterous, discarded as futile. But then as more hands were raised and lowered to the small table of vibrating drinks, laughter bowed to a litany of hypotheticals, then an array of precedents, to a synopsis of recent Cowopolis misfortune, to a slippery interpretation of the word as it applied to federal law; finally settling upon the silent, fallow fields of hope.

"Treason," Usurper repeated it for a third time. The word brought with it a mystical, magical quality, as though bugles for a cavalry were sounding off. If the citizens of Cowopolis only knew the champions of righteousness working to resurrect them from the dead, the tears they might weep.

The mayor coughed, his face turned deathly pink. Hyantite sat looking straight ahead to the road, afraid to move or speak or think about what was being considered.

"Treason," Usurper said again, changing the inflection, as if by saying the word in multiple ways he could come to know it better.

"Isn't that what this is?" the man from New York said.

The three sat not knowing how to respond, dumbstruck.

"But. . . treason," the mayor said. "You said *treason.*"

"I know I said treason. I said it because that's what we can make this."

"It's unthinkable."

"Nothing's unthinkable, mayor."

"It's despicable."

"That's irrelevant."

"To you. But I run this town. It's not irrelevant to me."

"Mayor," the man from New York said, pushing his glass aside with his forearm, creating a space where he could move his hands, "you hired us because you're in a jam, right? Right. If you weren't in such a big jam we wouldn't be here. The way I see it, the law is there like this great big ocean. It's just there. I don't know how it got there, but it's there. Now some people let that big ocean hold them back. It's too big. It's too dangerous. Scary— *ooooooh.* Other people, people with some imagination and know-how, they look at that great big ocean as an opportunity. An opportunity to take them places. To carry them off to a *better* place. That's where we come in. Think of us as a boat. One of them nice pretty yachts you see lined up in Palm Beach. We'll take you any place you want. All you have to do is have a little faith, some imagination thrown in, and we'll get you there."

"Sounds all too good," the mayor said. "Where did you learn this stuff?"

"Frank," Usurper said, "he's just trying to help."

"Oh, is that what he's doing?"

"Yeah, that's what he's doing."

"Have some imagination, a little bit of faith," the mayor muttered, looking out the window.

"Why not?"

"Because it stinks, that's why not."

"What's the alternative?" Usurper asked. "We've been tossing this around all morning. This is the best thing I've heard yet."

"Theo, did you hear what the man said? Did you hear it? He said treason. *Treason,* Theo."

"I know, Frank."

"That's crossing the line. Lord knows I am what I am, but that's crossing the line."

"Is it though?" Usurper said, taking a drink, leaning forward to look past Hyantite beside him, to the mayor who sat in a small, worried ball in the corner. He waited to make

37

eye contact, but the mayor just stared out the window.

"You know it is," the mayor said.

"I know we have to do something."

"God, Theo," the mayor said grabbing his hair, "what are we doing?"

"Easy, Frank, take it easy."

"How can I take it easy? Look at us. Treason," the mayor said to himself. "Why that's punishable by. . ."

"Death," Hyantite finished for him.

"Yes," the man from New York said. "I thought we all understood this?"

"We do," Usurper reassured him.

"Doesn't sound like your mayor does."

"He does."

"We don't have to do this, you know."

"He'll be all right. Keep the man driving."

"Sure, I can keep the man driving. We can drive around all day if you like. But what's the point if you guys are going to back out on this?"

"We're not backing out. Don't worry."

"Worried?" the man chuckled. "I'm not worried. I'm just trying to save the ozone here because there's no point going round and round like this if you people don't have what it takes to carry this thing out. Worried? I ain't worried."

The man from New York looked at his watch, then shook his head. He looked to the man from Washington. The Washington man was all of twenty-five. He moved only to breathe, or redirect his eyes, or now to speak in slow baritone logic.

38

"The question here is, what has your Jerry Wrigdd fellow done? It's not our job to judge this man. His guilt or innocence exists independently from us. What we're proposing here is simply to charge him, which in many ways is a duty you have as leaders of a dying city.

"What has he done? Has he intentionally sought to undermine your team's ability to play here in Cowopolis, Mr. Usurper, your law and order, Mr. Hyantite, and your city in general, Mr. Mayeye? The answer to this question is, of course, yes. The questions then follow: Have these actions attacked the very fabric of Cowopolitan society; was it their intent to extract the social and economic life-blood out of this city; was it this man's intent to drive professional football from Cowopolis and in doing so injure, perhaps critically, the body of professional sports in a broader sense; was it part of his design to wound the nation itself, were his actions sabotage against the State; did he intend to erase accepted Americanisms, what this country stands for, what its people have fought for, what it *is*? The answer to these questions, gentlemen, in my opinion, is yes. The only remaining question is whether a jury in a court of law will reach the same conclusion. But I remind you, that's the responsibility of the courts. It's not the responsibility of anyone in this limousine. Your hands—and here I direct my attention to the good mayor's comments—will drip no blood if he is convicted."

"However," the man from New York quickly added, "in all likelihood it won't come to that. Your man, when faced with this, will probably let it go."

"If he's smart," said the Washington man.

"If he's smart, agreed."

"He is that," Usurper said.

"Good, then he'll come around."

"He's smart, but he's different."

"They're all different," the New York man said.

"No, not like him. I've never met anybody like him."

"Yeah? Bet I've met a thousand guys just like him."

"No, you haven't."

"Bet I've met a thousand guys on my block just like him."

"Well, then, Mr.—what was your name again?—if that's true then you know there's a very real possibility that he won't give in. There's a very real possibility he'd rather face the chair than give in."

"Then there's the very real chance he'll fry," the New York man said smiling.

"That's what we've been trying to *tell* you," the mayor said from his corner. "Jesus, what are we doing here. What am I doing here. . ."

Usurper tapped his lips and gazed out the little hole he'd smeared on the window, watching the orange barrels flash by, thinking about the word.

Jerry Wrigdd moved against the cold that slapped at his face, through the snow which like a lover could be warm, or vague, or playful, or fatal, into darkness with its sounds and mystery and isolation. Into a world of slowing cars and rummaging dogs. He walked at times without knowing where he was headed, or where just two minutes before he had been. Without feeling his limbs, without feeling his muscles or bones or organs digesting bits and pieces of meals reluctantly offered to a listless mouth, without feeling the numbness growing, or the danger, or the damage. He stopped in small quiet places which drained him of sobriety, money, hope. Some of these places were like wax museums, and they had people in them who moved only when movement was compulsory; they sat scattered around in the gloomy ether as though expecting something, or someone to arrive. Others had people laughing and drinking in them, as though the world was a good place. Wherever he went, he was left alone. He felt worse with each new drink, in each new corner, at each new quiet place. He picked at the labels on the beer bottles, he watched the nowhere unfolding around him. He found faces in the nowhere which looked as though they could be his face in ten or twenty years, if he were to live with the walking dead, beyond the beyond which he feared more than anything—despair without any memory of hope. He left each place as he had arrived, having been given no hello, or good-bye, no eye contact, no tilt of the head, no thanks, no see ya later.

He wandered through the old arcade. Most of the shops were closed. The tired old men and women who kept their shops open sat on stools staring out just inside the invisible lines marking their spaces, like defeated animals who had lost the courage to escape. He wondered why they were there. Why weren't they home with families or friends. Why were they here in this cavernous place with only wandering drunks like himself shuffling by. He found nothing in the arcade. He lingered, but nothing came, and

he left. The outside was a shock to his senses, and for a
brief time he remembered danger, fear, pain, until he was
numb again and could not be counted on to say why his feet
moved at all. The cold was vast, endless, like the stars
above him. He liked that. He liked being insignificant in an
endless universe with gods and eternity and aliens, rather
than in a place that closed in on you and urged you to drink.
His feet took him over paths in the snow that were worn by
thousands of day people. They took him across clean banks
of snow which someone the next day would notice and
wonder who had plunged into the bank, and what for, and
where to, and why hadn't he simply gone around.

He was crossing the street when two figures lunged at
him from the shadows. They came from different directions
jumping at his legs and head, and once he was on the
ground they began kicking him and beating him. He curled
into a ball. The first second he thought he was going to die.
The second second he thought he was going to live, but
would be an invalid the rest of his life. The third second he
knew they were amateurs, he felt ashamed not to be fighting back, ashamed to be subjected to boots and fists without retaliation. By the tenth second he again thought he was
going to be dead by morning, that he had underestimated
the capabilities of amateur murderers. They might have
killed him if the flower he had been carrying beneath his
coat had not fallen out. He'd bought the flower at the
arcade. It was a single daisy, her favorite kind. He bought it
with the vague intentions of placing it on her grave. He
went mad. He beat one attacker in the face with a nearby
hunk of concrete. The other one tried to run, but he tackled

him, stood above him and while holding the man's forearm with both hands, kicked between the hands until he heard the bone crack like a small tree limb.

"Unlucky," he said. "You jumped a man with nothing in this world to lose. I have nothing. I am nothing. I care about nothing. I might just kill you. I don't care. Run now, if you want to live!"

The man, without thought to his accomplice, took off down the street and disappeared into the farthest point of pink light. The other one, who now had a crushed face, struggled to stand up. He held his face, moaned, then fell back to the curb.

He found the head of the daisy and took it delicately in his hand. He found the stem, and leaves which were pressed into the snow from the struggle. He dropped them carefully into the pocket of his coat and then gently slipped his hand beneath the fragments. He held the hand still as he walked. He walked up Erie Street, to the Carnegie Bridge where the two stone giants greeted him with silent empathy. He did not pause to look up and wonder at them, but instead lowered his gaze and stepped straight onto the massive iron bridge. When he was a boy, snow was a spaceship which carried him to worlds of happiness, infinity, promise. He spent hours alone in the snow—happy hours—while other boys played together or fought one another. Snow was his friend and teacher. He talked to it, he believed in it, he understood many of its mysteries. The snow on the Carnegie Bridge could have been mud, or sand, or manure. It meant nothing to him.

As he neared the crest of the bridge the wind came

flying at him. He pulled his collar up, and pulled down his hat. He leaned against the wind as the snow pelted his face, and as he stood there he looked down to the river slowed by winter, its fringes congealed, its waters barely moving. The river had once been beautiful. It carried them on hot summer days, they walked along its bank, sank in its mud, stripped beneath its willows and made love in the sun. They picked dandelions which for two weeks in April were out by the millions. They watched boaters—drunkards and whores and important men—troll back and forth, all with a single purpose but different means, salmon of civilization. They ate berries and read books and wrote letters and hummed songs and made love often, unseen in the brush, emerging hungry and tired and damp and hot. He felt as though he would fall or jump. The river had been beautiful.

VII

"Jerry?" Mary Green called out, but there came no answer.

She looked in the kitchen, in the front room, and the downstairs bath.

"Jerry?" she called again.

The upstairs bathroom light was on, but he wasn't in it. As she turned to go into his bedroom she saw red plaid balled in a corner, and above the red plaid a tuft of dark hair, and below the hair a pair of eyes recessed in a sallow set of cheekbones.

"Jerry," she cried out, and fell upon him, sobbing.

She turned up the heat, rubbed his limbs, then sobbed again. She heated some soup, sliced two bananas in neat wheels and laid them around the bowl of soup, and fed him while he tried to smile. He reached out a cold hand to brush her cheek. The softness and color of her skin fascinated him. He wanted to capture the softness and color in his fingers.

"What's the matter with you?" she sighed.

"I don't know," he said looking down.

"What's happened to you?"

He couldn't say.

"Jerry, your head," she said, noticing the gash for the first time.

"Last week," he said.

"Oh, Jerry."

"It doesn't hurt anymore," he said, forcing a reassuring grimace.

"You fool."

"I know."

"And you didn't get it stitched. You know it's going to heal badly."

"You can't really see it, see, if my hair's down."

"You're an idiot."

"I can't help it," he said.

She shook her head. The tears came again.

She curled beside him, they fell asleep. She roused him in the middle of the night and put him to bed. He moved often, twitching, mumbling, seemingly in the midst of some disturbing dream. She slept very little. She loved lying beside him, and found agony in it. She wanted to feel his hand on her cheek again; on her nose, lips, hair. She wanted his hands to know all of her warm skin. She wanted his lips and straw hair and worried eyes and helplessness. *I pray for you, Jerry Wrigdd, heart of hearts, lost soul. I pray you will find what once was easy, and is now impossible. I pray you will find strength, hope, fire. I pray you will return, some-*

how, before it is too late.

"Mary," he called out to her the next afternoon.

"I'm here," she said. She came down and sat next to him on the bed.

"Where is your hand?"

"Here," she said. He took her hand and put it against his chest fiercely until he fell asleep.

"Mary," he cried out again two hours later.

"Yes," she said, and rubbed the back of his hand with her thumb.

"I can't move."

"You're tired," she said. "No, more than tired. You're not well."

"Everything is gone."

"What do you mean?" she said, pretending not to understand.

"I can't move. I can't see. It's all gone."

"You're too weak now. Rest. Don't even try. You need to get well again."

"But you don't understand. I can't see a thing. It's all gray."

"It will come back," she said to him.

"Are you crying?"

"No."

"What if it doesn't come back?"

"It will," she said, "it has to."

"But what if it doesn't?"

"Don't think of that," she said. The bed made small jumps from her crying.

"Mary," he said, reaching out for her.

47

"I'm still here," she said, squeezing his hand.

"Mary, where are you?"

"I'm right beside you."

"She's gone," he said, his voice less than a whisper.

"I know. I know she is."

"She's gone and I can't move and everything is gray."

"Don't be afraid, I'm here."

"I am afraid."

"Of course you're afraid, but it will be all right. You have to believe that."

"Hee—hee—hee, oh sure," he chuckled to himself. It frightened her.

"It will," she insisted.

"Hee—hee—hee. . . it all works out in the end. . . hee—hee—hee. . . I see. . . now I feel better. . ."

"Sure, you *will* feel better. Just give it time."

"I don't believe those things," he said. "I think I used to. I can't remember. I feel as though I did, but I'm empty. The gray."

"Are you hungry?"

"I'm dead. I'm not a living thing."

"No, you're not," she shook him. "You're alive!"

"I'm dead."

"You're alive and you'll get through this."

"I want to die," he said.

"Jerry, listen."

"I can't move. . . I can't see. . . I can't feel. Even the pain of losing her isn't real, it's just spilled gray. Everywhere there's the gray. I can't explain it. You don't understand. I'm dead."

He slept. She lay down on the floor with her coat pulled over her and slept soundly for several hours. She woke and found him still sleeping. His arms were in the air. Slowly he moved them. His arms moved in unison, they moved as the wings of a hawk, or some other great floating bird. She watched him, and then crept downstairs to clean the kitchen. He was awake and sitting when she crept back up to check on him an hour later.

"You're awake," she said, smiling now, standing on the threshold. Her rest had washed away much of her mental fatigue. She greeted him with newfound energy and hope.

"I just woke up," he said, staring blankly at the dresser.

"Are you hungry now?"

He shrugged his shoulders. "Mm."

"Thirsty?"

He shrugged one shoulder and curled the side of his mouth.

"Anything?"

"You shouldn't ask that to a man who's just woken up," he said wryly.

"Says who?"

"Says nuns and inmates everywhere."

"And virgins."

"Oh yes, the virgins."

"Can I get you anything?"

"Got any bagels?" he said, brightening up a bit.

"I doubt it," she said, trying to remember if she'd seen any. "You haven't been to the grocery lately, have you?"

"Aw, forget it," he said. "I'm not hungry. Bored, really. Isn't that why people eat, because they're bored?"

49

"They eat because they're hungry, Jerry. Do you re-member being hungry?"

"No, just being bored."

She crossed her arms and leaned against the door jam. She closed her eyes.

"Come here," he said offering her his hand. She opened her eyes, saw the hand, went to him and took it. "Look at you," he said, stroking her hair.

"What?"

"Nothing."

"What's wrong?"

"There's nothing wrong."

"See," she wrinkled her nose, "I told you."

He interlocked his fingers with hers. He stared into the blanket.

"Jerry, you're in trouble," she said.

He lifted his head and listened.

"They want to try you for treason. Do you hear me? Do you know how serious that is?"

"It doesn't matter," he said. "Treason? That's funny."

"Are you crazy? You'll go to jail. Or. . ."

"I know what you're saying, Mary, but you see, I don't care."

"What?"

"I said I don't care."

"It's your *life*, Jerry."

"What's left of it."

"You've got to get yourself a lawyer," she continued. "I know you don't want to sell the property, but you have to. It's the only way."

"I can't," he said. "You know that."

"I know I don't want to see you dead, because if you're convicted that's what you'll be."

"Good," he said.

"You don't mean that," she said, and for the first time the full impact of his words were absorbed and understood. It was an impossible statement. Yet, there it was; he'd said it. She took her hands away, and folded her arms across her stomach. "Jerry?" she said meekly.

He lowered his head, ashamed, unable to help himself.

VIII

You don't know him, I forget. If you did you would be as stunned as Mary Green, as stunned as I. But you don't know him. You never saw her. You never saw them. You can't understand the significance of it, when he looked up weakly into Mary Green's wide eyes and said the words, *I don't care.*

Those who knew him best have spent nights pondering the cause of his collapse. Men rise, men fall, it is the ebb and flow of generations. But when wizards tumble, when mystics lose themselves, it gives cause for serious reflection.

Some, including former friends, sit now in great leather armchairs and are laughing. This, I truly don't understand. Who would take pleasure in another's anguish, especially when that someone is a friend? I hear the whispering. I hear the snickering. I see the crooks in the corners of their mouths. He's taken it too hard, they say. He should have been over her a long time ago. It's all too embarrassing. Weakness, in the short term, is endearing, it's an expected reaction against the tidal wave of suffering. But over time, it becomes unsightly. The agony is supposed to disappear, magically. To you I say, you have not loved the way *he* loved. You have not known the twining of the heart. You will never comprehend the sublime meadow dance that lies beyond the moat of sexual stuttering—for it is like trying to convey death to the living, light to the blind, God to the disbelieving. This bonding is impossible to relate, it can only be experienced or not experienced. It is neither sought nor necessarily wanted, nor predicted, nor understood, but it is real. It happens to those whose hearts beat like drums, and to those who thought their hearts beat no more. It is indiscriminate, as any other disease or miracle, and when it comes there is nothing to do but go with it—for it will take you nonetheless, against your will, or better judgement, or preparation—it is the river, navigated but never ignored, and surely never defeated.

This man went down river with both arms digging. Few have given themselves to it so willingly or fully, and fewer still master so quickly its power. He went fearlessly. His aggressive strokes through subtle eddies, sudden turbulence, great falls, shaped him body and soul, and he emerged after a time a man like no other. I have seen many men in love, but have witnessed nothing like his love for her. I have seen more doting men, more affectionate men, more passionate men, but have never seen a man give more of himself than this man. He seemed nourished by it. The act of loving her enriched him. Time spent with her made him glow, like sunlight on a leaf. This abandonment, this receiving by giving, this supernova love, makes most shudder. To some it even repulses. So far have we fallen.

Jerry Wrigdd was no radical. He was a lover. He was a lover who could not be swayed by slick words, comforting reassurances, or denials, to stop loving. He has travelled far behind us, he has gone ahead already, eyes wide open. He knows what will happen a hundred years from now, or what could, or what must not. He sees things. He is able to mute the gibberish. He has no ego, and therefore no chains. He has no fear, and therefore no agenda. He has no immovable beliefs, and thus no manipulation of truth. He is able to hold in his hands the heart of another, he feels the pulse, the warmth, those inside battering their way out. He understands how this thing, the heart, is subject to cause and effect, caprice, inconsistencies. He understands the inertia of the heart once harbored east, or west, or ten fathoms under. The fates of others course through him like blood. She, his roof from the storm of storms. She, his voice in a sea of mutes. She, his hope amidst a culture in meltdown. She, companion on a lonely planet. Perhaps there it is, the answer: why wizards tumble.

IX

Mary lay in the tub, blowing on the water, thinking with eyes closed of another place not so long ago. She looked up through the rising steam to this man who stood in four-day-old underwear, face jutted toward the mirror. Slowly, cautiously, as though he had never before performed the task, he attempted to shave his face. She wondered how it had come so far so fast. She wondered why so few had jumped from the train. She wondered how this man could do anything for anybody. She slipped farther into the water, detaching herself from the reality before her.

It was only a hearing, she reminded herself, not a trial. He wasn't even required to attend.

"You don't have to go," she thought aloud, rising up on a crest of bubbles, moving her fingertips across the water.

"No?"

"Stay here with me. We can rent another Alfred Hitchcock movie."

"We could do that," he said, scraping the razor along his chin, down his neck, then up the side of his cheek to his ear. "Haven't we seen them all?"

"There's tons we haven't seen. I can make a roast. I'll make mashed potatoes."

"Mashed potatoes," he said. "Mm. I love mashed potatoes."

"We'll go for a ride. Get away from this place. I can take some time off—I've got it coming, you know. We're slow anyway."

"A ride," he said, his razor stopped. He thought of all the possibilities. He remembered the distant feel of hot sunshine on his skin. He remembered faces. "Yeah. We could do that. Go somewhere far away. It's a big country, you know."

"Jerry, they're waiting to butcher you."

"I know," he said matter-of-factly.

"And you're going to go."

"And I'm going to go."

"But why?"

"I think we *have* seen all the Alfred Hitchcock movies."

"But not all the Humphrey Bogart movies."

"No, not all the Humphrey Bogart movies," he said.

"Why are you doing this?"

"What else can I do?"

"Anything," she said. "Anything else."

"It might be fun," he said, turning his head, "I'm kind of looking forward to it."

"Why are you so stubborn?"

"I don't know."

"You're a mess. Look at yourself. They're going to butcher you."

He paused to look at himself in the mirror. He saw unknown features, distorted, exaggerated, shrunken. It was his face, but that was not him.

She rose from the bath, beautiful, wanting to smile, wanting to take him away to a place before or after or could have been, to a haven of sanity, to the garden of souls. He had described it once. It was a place of serenity, of power, a haven where those who are sick can heal, can become what they once were, or what they desire to be. He said he could not describe it accurately, but it was real. She fell against him, wet, afraid. He held her, and in holding her a forgotten bliss returned for a moment. He wished there was another way.

There was a knock at the door. He opened it to find two men in trench coats standing on his stoop. They took him to a waiting car. As the car moved through familiar streets he peered out a small hole he had rubbed on the window. He felt himself being taken by the river, and in that submission there was an unburdening, but there was nothing waiting to carry the unburdening, and so it fell quickly and heavily onto the desert of his consciousness.

City hall came into view. Temple of law, order, justice. Starlings moved across the lawn in noisy, erratic bunches, through the hedges to light on patches of salted sidewalk where there was bread and sometimes french fries tossed by new office clerks or sanitation men on lunch break.

The car stopped. There was no getting around the mob. The door was opened for him. He was wedged between two bodyguards who pushed forward like dual icebreakers. Through the gaps between bodyguards, beyond the crust of reporters and cameramen, he saw stocking caps pulled low, framing pink faces and bared teeth and crazed eyes. He covered his face as snowballs were hurled at him. He told himself this wasn't happening. These people weren't gathered here to heave snowballs at *him*. It couldn't be.

When they reached the statue of Herbert Horatio Steele, their forward movement was stopped. He looked up. A banner had been draped across the statue, it read *Death To Traitors*. A crowd of youths was encircled about the statue chanting, "Death to traitors! Death to traitors!" He covered his eyes, then ears, then eyes, then shouted as loudly as he could, but no one heard above the chanting. Images of inquisitions past flashed before him. The beast which knew no bounds in space or time shook the earth and laid waste to sanity. "Death to traitors! Death to traitors! Death to traitors!" they chanted as he was led up the final steps and taken inside.

He was made to wait outside the chamber. The wide old hall was cold, and unusually dusty, as though the dust were never removed but was pushed to other halls leading to other chambers. Two young aides strode across the hall carrying stacks of bouncing paper. They knocked on the chamber door. As they waited he could see the flirtation going on between them, and he knew who the catalyst of the flirtation was. He remembered what it once felt like to be like them, working toward something clean and promising and templated.

"Mr. Wrigdd?" a man suddenly appeared from inside, propping the door open with his foot.

When he stepped into the chamber, those whispering stopped their whispering. Those sitting up above in the steep balcony sat on the edges of their seats jerking their heads for a better glimpse; mothers pulled children close. Most had not seen him in the flesh. Some recoiled as he walked by, as though a lion or bear were being led past.

In the center of the chamber was a long table. Around it sat men and women in gray suits, with tired but ravenous eyes. The way they were squeezed in around the table made him think of Thanksgiving as a child, and how the adults squeezed into any gap they could find to avoid sitting at the little table with him and the other children. As he approached, those with faces pressed to yellow tablets lifted them with casual interest, like feeding beasts. Those with heads in hands sat up, stretched their necks against tight cloth, moved their eyes sluggishly. They introduced themselves, and as they did he lapsed into a daydream. He wondered what kinds of pets these people owned. Chocolate labs most likely. There was nothing wrong with chocolate labs, except when connected to things like these sitting around a giant table, bored with the business of crucifixion. He thought how those dogs would never see their masters introducing themselves politely, even warmly, to a man they were about to dismember.

"Jerry," said a man who sat directly across from him; he spoke in the most pleasant mourning dove coo, all coconuts and cream, wearing the gentle countenance of a philanthropist. This man had an unusually kind face, a cherub face, a youthful, acne-scarred face, with smooth black hair and eyes that seemed only temporarily stuck to his sockets, like maturing larvae. The smooth quality of this man nearly made Wrigdd feel privileged to be sitting across from him. He had, like some of the others, a little pyramid of cardboard in front of him. The little pyramid of cardboard read: *Chairman Manny F. Destiny.* "I trust you made it through that zoo out there without any problems?" he asked in the smooth voice.

Wrigdd shrugged.

"Fine, that's just fine," the man said. "Jerry, do you know who I am?"

He looked around him at all the long, gray faces. He wanted to laugh, but found it hard to laugh at lethal absurdity. "I'm fairly well-acquainted with American history," he replied.

"The insolence!" came a shout from the gallery.

"Sit down, sir, and be quiet," Destiny said sternly to the man.

"You, you. . . nothing! Who do you think you are? Mr. Zero!" The man shook his fist and contorted his face. He was promptly removed from the chamber.

"Jerry," Destiny said, "you're a smart boy. I've heard you're a real sharp whip, all right. Good. I like smart people. Jerry, let's get down to it, shall we? We've asked you to come on in, hoping you might shed some light on a few things. That's what this is all about. That's why all these people are here.

"Jerry, I understand your uncle, Mr. Adam Selowt, owns

a piece of property in downtown Cowopolis. This piece of property—am I right about that, Jerry? You listen real close now and tell me if everything I say is correct—okay, Jerry? This piece of property he agreed to sell, in good faith, to Mr. Theo Usurper, principal owner of the Bovines, for the price of twenty million dollars. These two gentlemen came to an agreement, I note, having not actually signed the legal document, but nonetheless having reached an agreement in principal. This property is, from all indications, the only viable piece of property in the Cowopolis metropolitan area where a new stadium could be built.

"On the night of August third, your uncle suffered a debilitating rupturing of a cerebral aneurysm. Jerry, I'm just going over the sequence of events here, you let me know if I'm going too fast. Chime in whenever you like. Prior to this, your uncle signed power of attorney over to you. Soon after your uncle became incapacitated, you were to exercise your newly acquired power of attorney and sign the property agreement. You declined to do so. Over the months, Mr. Usurper and his attorneys tried to meet with you, in an attempt to resolve your differences. You repeatedly made yourself unavailable for dialogue.

"In the roughly, oh, six month period since that early August day, Cowopolis has become a different city. There has been civil unrest, rioting, work stoppages. Domestic violence has increased. Public intoxication, school truancy, illegal gambling—all have been burgeoning. We've been told that business leaders are nervous about workers leaving, and prospective employers are turning away, they're moving on to other cities. People are frightened.

They're afraid of what's going to become of their lives. They're afraid of their future. They're afraid of their own neighbors. Cowopolis, so I've been told, once was an ideal place to live. Now, why it's falling apart. The city has drifted into a sort of catatonic despair."

Destiny paused to rub his eyes and take a drink. "Jerry, we're here to bring out the facts, get everything out in the open—no secrets here. In particular we want to hear your side of the story. I'm not going to lie to you," he said somberly. "You could be in a heap of trouble. If the facts pile up mostly on this side," he said, holding up a large, puffy mitt, "then we toss this whole thing out. Gone. You're a free man. We apologize for any inconvenience we've caused you. But," he said, his eyes cast downward, as though it hurt to say the words. He fumbled with the corner of his nameplate, then lifted his eyes again. "But, if the facts pile up mostly on the *other* side, then it will be this committee's recommendation that you be charged with treason against the United States of America, for which the severest penalty, upon conviction, is death. Are you comfortable, Jerry? Paul, get him a glass of water, will you."

"Jerry, tell us in general terms what you were trying to accomplish by refusing to sell the property. What was your state of mind at the time?" Destiny removed his glasses, and sucked on one of the loops.

"What was I trying to accomplish?" Wrigdd said, casting his eyes to the walls, trying to gather his thoughts. He was afraid that if he looked at Destiny he might offer his head on a platter right then and there. "I had other ideas

62

for it," he said. I couldn't sell it." He stole a glance at Destiny, trying to superimpose the Grim Reaper over that benign, cherub face, but it just wouldn't go. "It's that simple," he said.

"Yes," Destiny said, shuffling through his papers, as though looking for some specific page, or piece of text, "we've heard. Can you tell us what you wanted to use this property for?"

"Sorry, but I can't."

"You can't?" Destiny replied, still shuffling, but then, momentarily, giving up. "Why can't you?"

"I just can't."

"A museum? A new library? Maybe a zoo? A mansion? Can't you tell us?"

"No, I really can't."

"Was it something your uncle would have liked?"

The doomed one laughed. "I don't think my uncle, you old whatever it was you tried to be with your life, would have understood. Let's put it that way."

"A personal use then?"

"I wanted to use the property for something better, if that's what you mean. Paul, more water please?" he said, shaking his glass of ice cubes.

"Something better than a new stadium?" Destiny said, narrowing his eyes, awaiting the implausible answer.

"I suppose I could have done worse," Wrigdd said, "with a New York City dump site, or a high security prison for first-time marijuana users, but I had a fair amount of leeway in the don't-fuck-it-up area, I do believe."

"Now that's funny, because most people around here are

in the opinion that you did just that."

"Really?"

"Really."

"Okay," he shrugged, "you win. Why, thank you, Paul."

"I'm serious, Jerry," Destiny said. "I'd really like to know all about this. . . *thing* you wanted to build."

"No can do," the dry-mouthed one said.

"I just don't understand."

"Because," Wrigdd said, "I might still build it." And with those words the chamber gasped in unison.

"You might still build it?" Destiny said, slapping the table, "why, good for you, Jerry. You're no quitter. I like your gumption. I like your style. But I don't see how telling us will change anything."

"It might."

"How could it?"

"I don't know."

"The land is yours, yours to do with as you like. Yours to build upon, yours to let lie empty. You don't think someone would want to stop you?"

"I don't know, but I can't risk it."

"Is it something offensive?"

"You're asking *me* that?"

"But don't you understand, son, that your evasiveness makes you look guilty of something?"

"Well, your persistence makes me suspicious of something."

"I think you're paranoid," Destiny remarked.

"Not me," the wide-awake one said.

"Jerry, let me ask you something else, because I see

we're not going to get any more out of you on this point," Destiny said, fumbling through papers again. He stopped. Both his hands were full. He seemed to want to ask a question so he could continue his search. "Do you feel any remorse for what you've done?"

"I don't know," said Wrigdd. "What have I done?"

"Exploited your uncle's position for personal gain, in direct conflict with his wishes, for starters."

"Hmm. . . no, I'm afraid my membership to the guilt society ran out years ago."

"You don't?"

"No."

"Bastard!" somebody howled.

"That will be enough!" Destiny shouted back.

"But he is!"

"Get that man out of here," Destiny said to the bailiff, pinching at papers, looking momentarily lost.

"You're going to rot in hell, Jerry Wrigdd," the man, wearing overalls and an old brown baseball cap, said. He pulled a screwdriver from the front of his overalls, pointed it at him, then jabbed at the air. "Mm—mm—*mm!*"

"So. . ."

"So."

"We were discussing your remorse, or lack thereof. Jerry, do you believe in right and wrong? It's a simple question."

"Sure," he answered.

"Then do you believe what you've done is right?"

"I do."

"Explain," Destiny said, plopping an exasperated mug in

a soft, plump hand.

"Look, my uncle wasn't too crazy about the stadium deal to begin with. He had money trouble. Like you-know-who. Why is it *they're* always the ones with money trouble? It wasn't anything out of hand, a few million I think, but enough where he thought he could get back on track by selling. He felt he had to. When my uncle had the aneurysm, and it became clear he wasn't going to come out of it, there was no longer any compelling reason to sell. If he could speak for himself, knowing what lies ahead for him, I don't think my uncle *would* sell. Not now. So you see I am, in my view, honoring my uncle's wishes."

"And it was at that point you decided to use the property for this mystery purpose of yours."

"Oh, you know, I'd been thinking about *that* for some time."

"Your uncle's situation, it could be viewed as a gift?"

"I'm like anybody else. I have ideas. Mostly they sit around, maybe they disappear. When an opportunity comes along, I take it."

"You said you might still go through with your plans," Destiny said. "What's stopping you?"

"Things," Wrigdd replied.

"What things?"

"Just things."

Destiny's face rose from his hand, his look of frustration now replaced by one of curiosity. "Oh?"

"Look, I'd rather not talk about it."

"Does it have to do with your girlfriend?"

"I said I'd rather not talk about it."

"Jerry, I don't mean to upset you. I press only because that's why we're here, to find out why you've done what you've done. It might help us both if you told us what happened."

"There's nothing to the story," he said.

"She died last year, I'm truly sorry. I understand you had a special relationship. Can you tell us about it?"

"Ask me in ten years."

"She was going to help you with your project?"

"She was."

"And when she died you felt you couldn't go on with it alone."

He nodded, weakly.

"I suppose that could explain your reluctance to meet with Usurper, or at least partially explain it. It was probably the last thing on your mind," Destiny said. "I think I understand you on that point, Jerry. I think we all do." An aide whispered in his ear. Destiny nodded, listened, nodded, listened. The aide scooted back, a frail specimen he was, dominated by a heavy book which rested on his erect knees. "Jerry, tell us will you, was it your intent to move the Bovines out of Cowopolis," Destiny said, casually waving his glasses about, "was this something you wanted to see occur? Or was it a mere consequence, a. . . what did you call it?" he whispered to the frail aide.

"A casualty."

"Hmm? Speak up, can't hear you."

"A *casualty*—"

"Oh, right. Or *casualty* of the circumstances?"

"I'm sorry? I wasn't listening."

"The Bovines, I wondered if you might tell us how you felt about the Bovines. How did you feel about the new stadium. I'm trying to understand your motivation."

"My motivation?" Wrigdd said, giving it some thought. "I wanted to use the land for something else. Remember?"

"And the Bovines?"

"What about them?"

"Did you have an opinion one way or the other about them getting a new stadium, or whether they remained in Cowopolis?

"Sure, I did," he said.

"Which is? . . ." Destiny gritted his teeth and beckoned for an answer with his hands.

"If I tell you my opinion, you'll know how I voted," Wrigdd said, wagging a finger.

"By not telling us, we'll know how you voted but without the reasons why. It's the reasons why that might keep your body on terra firma, son."

"What the hell," Wrigdd said wearily. "All right. I thought it was about the biggest waste of four hundred million dollars I didn't want to be part of."

"I see. And why was that?" Destiny mechanically chomped on a wafer of ice.

Wrigdd shook his head. "Man," he said. "Do you know what I could do with four hundred million dollars?"

"I know there are a lot of frightened people who don't want to find out."

"Four hundred millions dollars. I mean, I can't even imagine what that is. I can do a lot with a hundred, a hell of a lot with a thousand, let alone four hundred million dollars. Maybe to someone in *his* shoes, that's peanuts, just chump change. But to someone with imagination, to someone like me. . . That's a sort of infinity."

"I take that as a 'no' vote?"

"Take it however you want."

"You have no feeling at all for the Bovines, do you?" And here, for the first time, Destiny felt he had lost his tenuous hold on his guest's psyche. He'd had it, barely, but now it was gone completely. He felt tired, and saddened.

"I suppose I have what divorced people have," Wrigdd said, "which is not to say I have no feelings."

"But you watched the Bovines as a child, you grew up with them?"

"That's right. I did."

"You went to Bovines games most of your life—I have it right here—sometimes three, four, five games in one season?"

Wrigdd nodded in the affirmative.

"Even now you're seen wearing a Bovines hat as you walk the city?"

"It's a cold place," Wrigdd said, "and that's a good hat."

"Come on," Destiny said in disbelief, "you can't be serious."

"Give me a new one, I'll wear it."

"It means nothing to you?"

"I'm divorced remember; next to nothing."

"I just don't get it," Destiny said, staring at his guest, shaking his head. "I really don't get it."

"Ask them," Wrigdd said, looking up to the hungry, leering faces. "Ask them what it is they go mad for. Ask them what they wait in lines for. Ask them what the Bo-vines, *today*, represent to them."

"When they're up for treason, I'll ask them."

"The Bovines, Mr. Destiny, are dead. There's nothing left of what I knew, but names and colors. Names and colors. I've done my grieving already. You gotta move on in life."

"Dead? Why sure they're dead, son," said a straight-faced Destiny, "you killed them."

"It's been a long, slow death," said Wrigdd sadly. "The worst deaths are."

"Jerry," Destiny said rubbing his eyes, "you've lost me. I thought you had me, but now you've lost me."

"Names and colors, names and colors. If you think they mean anything, then how can you ever expect to under-stand? It's everywhere—you don't have to move! Look around. What do you see? Names and colors. That's what you see, that's all there is—names and colors. They used to represent things. But now there's nothing more to the symbols than the symbols themselves. Why am I the only person who can see this?" He stood up.

"Sit down, Jerry," Destiny said gruffly.

"Mr. Destiny," Wrigdd cried out, climbing onto the big wooden table, walking on his knees toward him then stopping, his arms offered in placation, "It's so God damn obvious. What's wrong with you all? Have you lost your minds? Have you lost your consciences? Have you lost all connection with who got you here?"

"Bailiff!" Destiny jumped back in his seat.

"Are you so sure of yourselves?" he asked.

Marco Polio

"*Baliff!*"

There was a break. The men and women seated around the table made a quick exit for the restrooms, where there was much laughter, backslapping, and reaffirmation of their purpose. As hands were flicked in sinks, paper towels were yanked from dispensers, ties were adjusted and chests were heaved upward, there were congratulatory smiles, and proud nods, a few solemn winces of regret, but mostly forward-thinking, self-assured gestures that you find in committees of these sorts, the plodding wheel of the way it is, the way it has to be, churning steadily against the tumultuous river.

Inside, Jerry Wrigdd sat without expression, staring out the windows, oblivious to the stares, chuckles, pointed fingers, or the inhale which brought the committee members back, scooting wooden chairs against dull linoleum, clearing throats, exchanging papers. Destiny, oddly enough, sat paperless, elbows on the table, his head hung low. He appeared to be sleeping, though he wasn't. He was thinking. Unlike the others, he was thinking about some of the things Wrigdd had said, and not only was he thinking about them, he was allowing the words to sneak past the barbed wire of his ego, title, and purpose. The image of Wrigdd suddenly coming toward him, begging, wild, was still fresh in his mind. It had frightened him, but only initially. He knew there was never any danger. He had seen enough crazy men in his time, and this man was not crazy. Without wanting to draw attention to himself, he slowly lifted his eyes. He glanced about the room. In a strange moment of

71

clarity he saw those in the chamber with him, his fellow men, as he had never seen them before. He heard whispers, and in the whispering came previously veiled intents, meanings, fears. He heard unsubstantiated rumors, outright lies, and mindless regurgitation of other mindless regurgitations. It was like being pierced with a needle, he cowered from the caustic sound: the sound of the wheel, and the greasers of the wheel, and the benefactors of its power.

Into the chamber came a man. "Oh," Destiny said to himself, still morose on the inside, but having lifted his physical self again to a state of practiced congeniality. "He's early."

The chamber, upon seeing this man, erupts. This man is known by every human being on the planet with a working television set. He is known by many names: Beautiful physique. Stylish dresser. Sexy eyes. Charitable heart. Brilliant playmaker. Shoe spokesman. He is sometimes, though more often not, known by other names: Casual drug abuser. Sexual predator. Deadbeat dad. High school dropout. His dirty names remain carefully wrapped within the good names of beautiful physique, stylish dresser, brilliant playmaker. He is by loose definition, if not official proclamation, the New God.

There's the walk. That walk. *His* walk. Arms of a tiger, grace of a cheetah. Youthful arrogance, darling smile. He waves to his worshippers, grins. He's so cute, so coy, so brash. If you and I could only be like Him. If everyone could only be like Him. The world would be better if everyone could only be like Him. He sets his dark, panther eyes on the diminutive Wrigdd. Slowly, cat-like, he slinks forward. Standing there at the head of the table, he stares, glares, scowls, challenges, but then suddenly in that little boy way of his the scowl melts, the brow lifts, the dimples appear. The chamber is on fire.

"Jerry," Destiny says, his scalp reared back, eyes alight, cheeks flushed, as happens when you are face-to-face with greatness, "some members of the panel thought we might benefit by a visit from a special guest. I believe you know A. Game, the Bovines' all-star, all-*world* wide receiver. Mr. Game is here to give his own personal insight into our little problem." That was all Destiny could muster. With a motion that was more contrition than mere deference, he gave Game the floor.

Game sat on the edge of the table beside Wrigdd, dwarfing those around him, swinging his Italian shoe back and forth like a metronome. Light seemed to emanate from him. The others seated at the table appeared dull, ordinary, and inconsequential in his presence.

He lowered his massive hand. "Jerry," Game said, "how you doin', man?" They shook hands.

"Doing Jim Dandy," came back the loathsome one.

"I hear you don't like football much?" Game said in a friendly way.

"Oh, I like football well enough," said Wrigdd.

"Me too," said Game, flexing his cheek muscles, giving him the dimples. "Football is a good game. Some folks like it better than baseball, basketball, better than anything. It's a good game."

Wrigdd waited for more, but that was it. He looked up at Game; the thought of Swiss cheese entered his brain and wouldn't let go. "I got a friend," he then said, "he likes ping-pong."

"Ping-pong," Game puckered his lip, pondering, "that's a good game too. You need wrist control for ping-pong, good eye-hand coordination. Ping-pong's a good game."

"Yeah, well, he'll sit in his underwear Saturday's and Sunday's, all day long, and watch it. His head goes back and forth, back and forth, like this. He's got a satellite dish. He doesn't leave the couch, except to use the bathroom during commercials. He's a ping-pong *nut*."

"That's a little strange," said Game.

"Yeah, well, you have to know Robbie. I got another friend who likes women's tennis. You like women's tennis?"

"Tennis? Yeah, tennis is a good game."

"I think so too. Well, Ronnie, he likes to watch those short little skirts flip up in back—*swooooosh!* He likes it when they go for a shot, and grunt, and the little white skirt flies up—*swooooosh!* Says the whole thing is about as sexual as an NC-17 movie, if you think about it. All those white panties flashing around the court, the grunting and sweating and sprawling, rumors of locker room hanky-panky; it really gets him going. He likes women's ice-skating too. They don't grunt or sweat so much, but they make up for it in the riding-up-the-crack department. Ronnie, he doesn't even know how to keep score in tennis, but he'll watch it every chance he gets. I wonder if he's a voyeur?"

Game scratched his head. "Maybe," he said.

"Yeah, well, I worry about the guy. Hey. I got another

friend, Rosie. She doesn't watch T.V. much anymore. I asked her how come and she said it was because she found herself sitting in front of the T.V. day and night flipping through channels like a maniac. I said, 'What's wrong with that?' She said, 'What do you mean, what's wrong with that?—It's a frigging waste of time.' She's a little odd, Rosie is. Anyhow, now she spends her time not in front of a T.V., but in front of a computer. Sits there all day long. Spends her time in chat rooms. I asked her why she doesn't chat the normal way with real live people, but she just mumbled something incoherent. She's been booted out of most of those chat rooms. She's always picking fights. Nobody wants to talk to her, so she starts getting nasty, and the next thing you know she's on the outside looking in. She changes her name every time she signs on. Man. What do you like to do with your spare time, Game?"

"Me?"

"You probably don't have that much time to spare, with all the training you do."

"Naw, man," said Game bashfully, "you know, we're always travelling, or playing a game, or practicing. But when I get a chance I like to golf a few rounds."

"That's right, I've seen you on some of those charity tournaments. Hey, you're pretty good."

"Well," said Game, the dimples.

"You know you are."

"A two handicap," he said modestly.

"Get out," said Wrigdd, giving him a playful shove. "Wow. That's great."

"Thank you."

75

"Yeah, I imagine with your schedule it's hard to find time to do much of anything. But a two handicap. Holy mackerel. . . Hey, Game, where are you from originally—Philly? I heard you were from Philly."

"Naw, man. I'm from Pittsburgh."

"Pittsburgh? Well, I'll be. I like Pittsburgh. It's got a great feel to it with all those bridges."

"It's all right," Game said noncommittally.

"Pittsburgh's a great steel city, all right. Think of all those rivets on all those bridges. Bet there's millions of 'em. Think of all that steel coming out of all those factories. Think of how hot it must have been working in one of those factories."

"My dad worked in one," said Game with a sudden prideful smile.

"You don't say?"

"Thirty-six years."

"Thirty-six years, in a *steel mill*. Now that's something. Your old man, you could say he helped build this country from the ground up."

"He always took pride in his work," said Game, noticeably distracted in thought. "Missed only three days of work in his whole life, and one of them days was when I was born."

"Thirty-six years," Wrigdd repeated. "Can't imagine it. You could say his sweat made it possible for you to be who you are today."

"Most definitely," said Game. "Oh, without a doubt. I owe my dad everything I got."

"Look at you now," smiled Wrigdd. "You, the son of a

steel worker; the greatest thing since sliced bread. Bet he's proud."

"Doesn't miss a game."

"From the pages of obscurity, to world-wide adulation. He still work?"

"Oh, no, man. I saw to that. Soon as I got my shoe contract, I told him to put in his notice. He and mom are living the good life now. Got 'em a winter home in Florida, send 'em on trips to Hawaii and Las Vegas."

"You're a good man," Wrigdd said, patting the giant on his back. "You don't forget where you came from. You take care of your own kind. You're a good man. They're lucky to have a son like you. *We're* lucky to have a shoe spokesman like you. And. . . what else is it that you endorse?"

Game, away in thought, snapped back to face a question which had answers long-ago memorized: "Well, I got the chocolate smackies endorsement, the soda pop, the underwear, ties, the casual wear line, the sports wear line, the jock itch, the deodorant, the mouthwash, the mutual fund, the automobiles. . ." He rubbed his chin, "Pizza, chicken, burgers, milk, combs, batteries, tires, *golf balls* of course, jackets, gloves, beer, condoms, laxatives, modular homes, cable—"

"Stop," said Wrigdd, "did you say *laxatives?*"

"Mm-hm."

"Then maybe you could help me out." He motioned for Game to come lower with a wiggle of his finger. "You see," he said in a whisper, cupping a hand to the side of the giant's face, "I have sort of a problem. I think it's stress-

induced, you know, being threatened with the chair and all;
it's got me a little, well, irregular. Do you think—"

"Man," said Game empathetically, draping his huge
limb around Wrigdd's puny shoulder, "I don't know
nothin' about that stuff. I rarely have the problem myself.
My granny used to say stewed tomatoes would undo you,
though. That and hot wings. Hot wings sure enough clears
her out. You sure you're drinking enough water? Six
glasses a day, they say."

"I drink four," Wrigdd said seriously.

"Not enough," Game shook his head.

"Does pop count? Two cans of pop a day, plus the four
glasses of water. Think that equals *five* glasses of water?"

"I don't know," said Game. "They say pop isn't the
same as water. I don't know."

The conversation went on more or less the same for a
good half hour. Surprisingly, the two men seemed enam-
ored with each other. It was just before Game had to leave,
when Wrigdd made a series of strange statements.

"You know," he said, "I've travelled around a bit
myself."

"I *love* travelling," said Game.

"Actually, I've done quite a lot of it. That's where I'd
get ideas for my poetry."

"You write poetry?"

"I used to."

"Ever thought of getting them published, put into a
book?"

"Naw," said Wrigdd dismissively. "Here? In *this*
country? What's the point?" he laughed.

Game laughed back. "Yeah, true."

"I've met millions of people," he continued, his voice lowering, eyes dark, glimmering with intensity. "I've met millions of people, and you know what?"

Game shook his head.

"None of them have heard of you."

This caught Game off guard. He obviously didn't know what to think. He didn't know whether it was some awkward sort of compliment, or. . . well, what else *could* it be. He sat on his hands and looked up to the gallery, uneasily. He half-expected someone to roll in a five foot cake—for it was very close to his birthday—or perhaps he was going to be given some new award, specially created for him.

"Yet," Wrigdd continued, "they know me by sight, instantly, even those whom I've never met. They understand who I am. They know why I'm there. They welcome me, and I am treated with kindness and warmth.

"The world is on its head," he said with a queer and distant gaze. He looked Game in the eyes. It was a disturbing look, one which Game would remember against his desire to forget. "The world is on its head."

"You're real funny," Destiny said after Game had left the room. He looked upon Wrigdd contemptuously. "You think this is one big joke, don't you."

"I wish it were," said Wrigdd without expression.

"Jerry, do you believe in *anything*?"

"I believe in sanity," he said. "I believe in what works. I don't believe in lies."

"Is that what you think of this?"

"More or less."

"Where do you come from? Were you dropped from a spaceship, or just dropped on your head; who do you think you are?"

"I know who I am," said Wrigdd, "I'm a nobody."

"You, an unemployed, good-for-nothing poet. Yet for some reason which escapes me, you take a swing at everything good and honorable. That's perverse."

"It is what it is. Call it what you want."

"I see. I see," said an embittered Destiny. "It goes—zoom!—right over your head. You just don't get it, do you? You know, Jerry, I thought I could come to understand you. I really did. Stupid of me, I now realize, but I thought if I really tried I could get inside that head of yours. Everybody told me I was wasting my time. It now seems they were right." He rubbed his face with his big hands, as though he had a washcloth. His face was red, his eyes flat. "My God," he said, "you've been lost this whole time. What do you think this is, son; the stadium, people like Game, the citizens who come out in droves to watch these proceedings. Do you have any clue what this is all about?"

"What's it all about?" Wrigdd said, dropping his head to think. He lifted it again. "Why, it's all about giving meaning to a generation who has none, isn't it?"

80

X

He had his nose pressed to the big cold window, looking out from the empty nook of the old bar, into the night with its parked cars and immovable street lamps, stiff winter shrubs, lost plastic bags, and the wind which came in gusts; he rolled his nose left and right, pulled away to look at the greasy imprint, smiled, actually laughed to himself because no one was around, and because he was almost—but not quite—drunk. He put his weight again on his nose and wondered about things like destiny, self-determination, and the omnipotent, omniscient, all-good Vacationing One. But in his altered state he probed only superficially, preferring to think instead of a cabin in the wilderness, candles, and a woman wrapped in wool. He looked down to his glass, moved his fingers one at a time away from the stickiness, and thought about going home. He could be there in ten minutes. He could be in his bed, beneath the wool blanket, alone, thinking of her until his enemy insomnia relaxed, looked the other way, and he mercifully was allowed to sleep. The alcohol would help, especially if he drank enough of it. He chuckled to himself. Things were now funny. They were profound. Possibilities existed where they did not exist before.

He turned around and there was the waitress, holding two pints. She held them high, rolling them in the air, shimmying toward him.

"You're not going to get into trouble?" he asked her as they slid into opposite sides of the booth.

"After last night they'd pay me to find out about you," she said. "Besides, it's not exactly like you need three waitresses working, what with two drunks in one corner, and two drunks in another corner, and one drunk, you, doing your statue impression in another corner." She slid back and pushed her feet up on the bench beside him. She lit a cigarette, and with one hand crumpled below her weary breasts and the other one holding the torch, blew terrific streams of smoke, steering the smoke away from him with an agile and somewhat large set of gray lips. "How many?" she said.

"Tonight? Not too many."

"Five? No, six?"

"Or thereabouts."

"You don't seem the alcoholic type."

"It's just a phase."

"I know. A six month phase."

"How'd you guess?"

"I'm a psychologist, remember?"

"You know, you look just like her," he said.

"I know, you told me last night. You showed me her picture. I don't look anything like her, except for our two arms and two legs."

"What are you talking about?" he said, swatting the air. "Here," and he took out his wallet and showed her the picture. She was standing beneath a tree after a rain, and sex, and quart of malt liquor, and skipped Friday classes. Her hair was damp, and limp, and she looked like every man's dream, the abandonment of love still in her eyes. "Hell," he said softly, "you could be her sister."

The waitress blew another perfect jet of smoke toward the coffered ceiling. "If you say so."

"Well, anyway," he said, stuffing the wallet back into his pocket. "You know, I don't know anything about you."

"I'm just like your girlfriend, except I don't look anything like her."

"You knew her?" he said hopefully.

The waitress laughed without the slightest body movement, except for the torch on her fingertips, and the lips. "I know me. I know you. It's easy enough to figure out who she was."

"I like your hair," he said.

"You really are drunk."

"It's beautiful."

"Keep that word in mourning," she said. "It has a meaning, which you've lost."

"Does everyone here think I'm crazy?" he asked, suddenly examining his hands, moving his fingers, then comparing the lines on his two palms.

"Oh, they don't think you're crazy. They just think you are what you are."

"What am I?" he said, still comparing his palms.

"Falling," she said.

He held his stomach and turned inward. He looked the way he normally looked with no one talking to him.

"Maybe you should think about going home," she said.

"I don't want to go home."

"You don't have to if you don't want to. You look tired, is all."

"I don't ever want to go back there."

"But it's where you live," said the waitress with a frown. "You do live somewhere, don't you?"

"Isn't the snow beautiful?" he said raising his face.

"Sure. I don't have to drive in it, you know. I just live around the corner."

"Did you ever listen to the snow?"

"Yeah, I hear it all the time. 'Terry, get your frozen butt home. *Terry. . .*' "

He pounded the table laughing.

"No, no, no. You're hilarious. No, oh God. . . Jesus." He took a sip from the pint. The pint registered no taste, only comfort.

"Tell me what the snow says," she asked him.

"The snow? It used to say things I can't remember now. Now it says you should have done this or you should have done that, or what are you doing to yourself."

"Are you sure it's the snow?"

"Who else could it be?" he said, looking at her.

"Maybe they're lost helium atoms looking for balloons

to fill."

"Maybe it *is* something else," he said contemplatively, his eyes big.

"There you go."

"You think I'm drunk, but the snow's been talking to me all my life. Oh, it's been talking up a storm these past few weeks. That's why I don't want to go out there."

He drank his pint, ordered two more, drank his, and then at her insistence started on hers.

"You're pretty good at that," she said.

"Like anything else, it takes practice."

"What's the matter?" she said, noticing a change in his mood.

"Nothing. I'm just thinking."

"Okay," she said, "I'm not going anywhere." She moved her crumpled hand from beneath her breasts, opened it and rested it on his arm. He liked having her hand there. It allowed him to open, when his natural inclination was to shut down.

"I was wondering, maybe you could tell me what's wrong with me," he said.

"You're drunk."

"I'm drunk because I'm defective. I know it."

"You're like anybody else," she said, shaking her hand.

"I'm not like anybody else," he said, shaking his head.

"Then *be* somebody else," she offered.

He looked at her. "I've tried. I'm a failure at it."

"I wasn't *serious*."

"Well, it doesn't work, not for me." He scratched at the table top, raised his head. "So what are you left with when you're defective, and you can't impersonate someone else, but you can't be you because you are a despicable aberration of mankind?"

"Hey," she said, shaking her hand again. "You're not despicable."

"I am what I am," he said.

"But you're not despicable," she repeated. He seemed not to hear her. She put her feet on his lap. "Will you rub my feet?"

"I don't know," he mumbled to himself, untying her shoes. He pulled them off. He pulled off her socks, but then after he did it he looked at her questioningly, and she moved her mouth into a pleasant smile to reassure him. "I just don't know anymore."

"Ugly, aren't they?" she said wiggling her toes.

"She had toes like yours, and they were beautiful."

"Jerry, she had beautiful toes because you loved her."

"Is that why?"

"Yes, that's why."

"Is this how you like it? I can't have my feet rubbed—I'm too ticklish."

"That's perfect," she said closing her eyes. "Just like that. Mmm, that's nice. . ." For a while he forgot about everything but the task at hand, and he suddenly viewed her feet as a momentary center to a transient universe. Their shape and size and movement and response to his rubbing were the core of his intellectual and physical purpose. Every bit of what he had left was put into satisfying them. "Is it true what you were saying last night," she said in a low, grateful purr, "about your travels?"

86

"What did I say?" he said, half-heartedly trying to remember.

"You said you were a famous world traveller, except right at the moment you hadn't let go of your anonymity."

"I said that?" he winced with embarrassment.

"No, I guess you wouldn't remember, considering your condition. But, do you remember telling us, after someone asked what airline you preferred, that you didn't travel by air, or boat, or car?"

"I didn't say I *walked* all the way around the world."

"You said you travelled through time," she said opening her eyes.

"That's funny," he said.

"Why is it funny?"

"It's just funny. Don't you think it's funny?"

"Is it true?" she pressed.

"I told you, I don't remember much about last night."

"Is it true you travel through time?"

"Maybe," he said.

"You sounded pretty convincing last night; what do you mean, maybe?"

"Maybe I do if you're different from most people, and maybe I don't if you're just another Einstein looking for a laugh."

"Do I look like an Einstein?"

"Einstein is everywhere, you can't tell so easily."

"So, it's true."

"Yes," he said without looking up. "It's true."

"My God. . ."

"You don't *believe* me," he said.

"Of course I believe you."

"Then you're crazy just like me."

"Of course I'm crazy, just like you."

"I'm a pathological liar."

"No you're not. You're tired of explaining yourself, that's all. You're tired of them laughing. You're tired of the craziness out there, and that's what's made you this way."

"You really are a psychologist."

"How do you do it?"

"The lying?"

"The travelling."

"I don't know. I don't do it anymore."

"What's the matter?"

"I don't know that either. I just can't."

"What happened?" But then she remembered. "Oh."

"That's right, the 'Oh' did me in."

"So you're grounded, so to speak."

"So to speak."

"But six months ago. . ."

"Six months ago I was someone else."

"Do you remember what you saw? Anything at all?"

"I remember things," he said. "I can't move, but I can remember."

"Tell me."

"All I had to do was close my eyes," he said, closing them.

"And then you saw?"

"And then I *moved*."

"Where to?"

"Anywhere."

"Were you more than an observer?"

"An observer? Oh, no. You don't understand."

"How long would you stay?"

"An hour, a day, a week, sometimes a year. Their time and our time are in no way connected."

"You lived in comfort, or squalor?"

"I lived, at different times, in most places. In squalor as often as not. In relative comfort and happiness as often as not. I landed with luck on my side as often as not, and made the best of my situation."

"What do you remember?" she whispered. "Tell me."

For a while he didn't speak, but sat motionless, eyes closed, his mouth moving silently. The images which were like indistinct apples upon distant trees moved closer, closer, until he was standing among them, where they were sharp, and bright, and within easy reach. There were so many he could not decide which ones to pick first. He organized them, gleaned the common currents running through each.

"I remember work," he began. "Plows which until very recently were pulled by horses and steered by hand, the sound of the blade scraping against rock, slicing the moist wedge, exposing the earth; the feel of that wooden handle in my hand, my hands becoming paws, the fingers permanently numbed at the tips; the contrast of my paws against soft linen or white, virgin skin. The feel of work in my back, and legs, and arms, so that you fall asleep at the dinner table with your paw curled around a cold saucer of milk. The ecstasy in rest, or even better, real pleasure. There was thirst, the parched throat, the relief of blessed water. I remember toiling until I could barely stand, in a factory, in a mine, beside a mule, behind the plow. The toiling formed me. It formed my body, it formed my mind. Toiling because there was no other way. Toiling for my own dreams, or more often by necessity for the dreams or perversions of someone else. Toiling, always toiling.

"There were points of heightened joy. A visit from a friend or neighbor. The smell of food. Rain in springtime. A fire in winter. A blanket against that same winter. Festivals of all kinds—drunken, dancing, senseless geysers which energized the soul and relaxed the grip of monotonous conformity; prancing, flirting, otherworldly celebrations, season to the meat and potatoes of life. I swooned at the sight of uncountable returning birds high in the air, going from horizon to opposite horizon; leaves in their slow explosions, snow in its swift demise; scents of honeysuckle, rose, and lilac, horse, hog, and whore, grazing, grunting, and sweating. I marveled at stars, which frightened me to fantastic beliefs. I was once a sailor, and the seas were continents of danger, promise, lust, greed, despair. I was a father, and lived my rebirth at the birth of my children. I was often a thief, and dumped the burden of my ways when fortune came knocking. The natural world tantalized my intellect; human civilization challenged my patience, beliefs, and sanity. These things pulled me to mountain peaks, regardless of my wealth, gender, race, creed, or ability.

"I remember physical beauty, physical contact, physical love. The first sight of female nakedness, the first smell of it, the first drop of it, the first lapping, the first grazing, the first weight of its undulations; the first plunging into, the first new world, the first awakening. Sighs, shudders, blasphemies unfurled beneath me like brilliant banners from sweet mouths, though I learned that the sound originated deeper, in an indefinable place, an organ with no name. Lilting, drilling, drifting to the newfound female forest filled with heroes, villains, violinists; pulling me in. There, I experienced sublime moments in earthly time. There, I lay with sculpture no artist could have made. There, I reversed the wheel, unleashed the dam, scribbled my page—the only page noteworthy—in the book of animal joy.

"I held love in my meaty paws. It took me on its ride, it bent me to its patterns. I fell drugged by its poisonous prick more times than I can remember, my insides scrambled, my mind altered. It made me jealous, it rendered me silly. It gave me courage, it gave me strength. It consumed my days with dreams and hope, it split my nights into hunks of restlessness. There was nothing unconquerable in its sights, nothing its fire could not sear. Nothing wealth could exchange measure for measure for, nothing torture could wash from its cloak. I once hid beneath deck, and sailed to far shores for this love. I fell from exhaustion toiling for its whims. I forfeited self-respect for its callous discontent. I spent a full ten years in simple bliss, favored by the gods, sucking its nectar. I dwelt unknown across the wall, seven years in Spartan exile. I died at its cruel feet, and withered into lonely solitude. I knew honest souls and puppeteers, happy warblers and scavenging crows, sowers and reapers. I knew these women separately, I knew them rolled into one. I found love in despair, in transit, in aisles and beneath weighty objects. Love does not float with the river, but spews its lava forth to change its course. It is the sculptor of our kind, around which all things flow.

"Then there was oppression, pestilence of human happiness. Man against child, man against woman, man against fellow man. It emanated from kings abusive with their lineage, legislators abusive with their ambition, managers abusive with their control. It erupted from husbands bound by artificial duties, who lashed out at those weaker. It was perpetuated one clan against another. It froze understanding into castes of varying shades. . . Oh, God—the horrors we do to one another in the name of goodness and righteousness! Everywhere it breaks men's backs, women's hopes, children's futures. Everywhere it comes, it lays waste to humanity.

"I remember walls, everywhere walls. Walls on sea-shores, walls in villages, walls in bedrooms, walls within walls. I saw these walls go up, propped by fears, maintained by more fears. I saw the simplicity of their application, the complexity of their effects. Walls arise one-sided defenses, in truth are two-sided barriers. That which safeguards, denies. That which allows, disallows. The thickness which gives strength, conscripts that strength. I have known these walls intimately, regularly, they are temples to loneliness, suffering, hatred, prejudice, defeat."

He collapsed onto the table. The waitress, holding the expired butt of a cigarette in her upturned hand, wanted to believe him. But she also heard the voices inside, and the voices working in the kitchen and behind the bar, and the voices on the street, and in the papers, and in the court-house who had confirmed his lunacy. She lit several more cigarettes and smoked them and did much thinking. When it was closing time she roused him, gently. She offered to take him home, but he said he couldn't go home yet, he wanted to walk around some because he loved the snow, it sang wonderful songs to him at night.

XI

I know you're watching. I know you're up there, but I can't see you, not clearly. I wake up each night, I can't sleep. I've tried the pills, but I'm afraid of them. I'm ashamed of who I've become. Sometimes I hope you can't see me. But then, if I think about it, I know you must know that I can't help it. You wouldn't recognize me. I've become someone else. Someone who lives alone, who never comes out, who has lost himself. Remember Aidan? That's who I've become. I am Aidan. Afraid of the world. Afraid of the pain. Having lost the will to hope.

Today, by my watch, it's Tuesday night. I'm lying in bed. I have a new apartment now. I couldn't stay in our old one after you died. I have my bed on the floor. I like it on the floor. I can hang my arms and legs over the sides and touch the floor, or read a book and have it close. The walls are white. I have our plants here in the bedroom. I've been thinking a lot here on the bed. I watch the birds. I am feeding them. I am feeding the outside cats too. I'm getting a little better as time goes on, though it doesn't seem like it from day to day. I go up, I go down. I'm afraid of what might happen.

I have a cold. It's better when I'm lying on my back. I can see the branches of the trees. With my eyes closed I think of our walks in the woods. How I loved you in the woods. You're so beautiful there. You're beautiful in sunshine, in rain, against the bark of trees, with crickets singing around you, stars at night above you, water running over you, your hair flying like a tornado around your face. I love to watch you when you don't know it. I am the luckiest man in the world. Sometimes I wonder why I'm so lucky. I don't know why you love me.

Though you wouldn't recognize me, there are moments when I'm whole, when my mind returns, and briefly I am the man you knew. My mind sharpens, my memory returns, there is lightness in my heart. I feel as though I am on the verge of travelling again—to sit with those desperate, doubting soldiers at Valley Forge; to stand for 12 hours at a time stooped beneath the sun, weeding tobacco rows; to clear vast forests with only axe and strength, and then plant precious seeds between the rolling hills of stumps. Time again becomes fluid, the tunnel opens, and I pass through it as before. It is beautiful, if only for that moment. It is fleeting.

I think of your body. Your body to me is proof of God. When I say proof I don't mean logical proof; I suppose I mean evidence. I've thought about it, and I believe God should not be looked for with logic, or with faith, but with eyes and ears and hands. I will think of your body in tandem with my own as I age, growing old with mine. You will be a beautiful old woman some day. You will have the clean, crisp lines of laughter and compassion on your face. Your skin will be mottled from days under our beautiful sun. Your eyes will be lively, your hands a little drier, a little slower, but rich in their history. I will lie with you as you age, on cold winter nights I'll warm you.

I feel as though no one else has gone through this before. Have they? Before, when I was there among them, I felt their pain. I felt their hollow cries in the night. I felt despair in its many phantom voices. But I never felt this. The past becomes obscure, just as the future. If the obscurity could be chased away and the lives of the people brought up again, it would be like pumping water from a well. People could drink from the aquifers of yesterday, and human suffering would fall away. You said before you were proud of me; I want to make you proud again. I will find the strength somehow.

You probably know about the trouble I'm in. It's all happened so fast. I understand what they're trying to do, but really I understand nothing. We are like two different species, I feel like an alien in my own country, on my own planet. I am trying to see from their perspective, but it's hard. They think I'm playing a game. You should talk to them and tell them how I don't play games. If just one person could see my sincerity. I wish I were somebody else. Sometimes it's like I'm in a dream, and when I'm dreaming things make more sense. It's like everyone vanished. I don't know who they are.

Mary has been with me. Without her, I don't know what would become of me. I may already haven fallen off the edge, into the bottomless pit. Pray for her. Not because I am dependent on her strength, which I am, but because she embodies everything that we struggled to become. She is, in flesh and blood, what words—however succinct or beautiful—can only crudely describe.

I remember The Way. The sheep, and rain, and hills, and fellow seekers, and you never complaining. I remember blisters on your ankles, and me too much the cattle driver. The ice cream, and Cadbury's, and pints in small country pubs. I found myself along The Way. The world was ours along its unmarked path. I was king, and you my harlot Sistine queen, through bogs and over heath. I wish they could walk that path, see what we saw, listen as we listened. What a strange and profitable thing that would be.

XII

Mary Green banged on the automatic door which would not open, yelling at the nurse inside. The door slowly split in two. She rushed in.

"Jerry Wrigdd! Jerry Wrigdd!" she cried frantically to the nurse.

"Calm yourself," said the nurse.

"Do you have a Jerry Wrigdd here? Look, he should be here—do you?"

"Just try and relax, Miss," the nurse, slow-eyed and thick-armed said, as she reached in front of her for some papers. "Let me check. What was his name again?"

"Jerry Wrigdd. Oh God. . ."

"Wrigdd. *Wrigdd?* That's a strange name; familiar though. How do you spell it?"

"W—R—I—G—D—D. Please, hurry."

"Ah," the nurse said evenly, pleased with herself for

finding the name, her thick, tight finger marking the spot.
"Yes. He was admitted this morning."

"Is he all right? Oh, God, please let him be all right."

"I don't know," the nurse replied. "Are you his wife?"
she asked without looking up, still reading along her
moving finger.

"He's not married. I'm a friend. Can I see him?"

"Just a minute."

The nurse called somebody on the phone, and that
somebody gave a lengthy discourse about *something.* "I
see. I see. Really? Oh, my. Oh, she can? Great. Hold on a
minute," and with that she covered the receiver and said to
Mary, "Miss? If you'll sign here you can see him now."

She took the stairs. On the third floor she found the
room. Another nurse, who resembled a crow in white,
called out from behind a desk as she lightly tapped on his
door. The nurse came flapping over.

"Miss? You're here to see Mr. Wrigdd?"

"Yes, I am," Mary said.

"Have they told you about him?"

"No."

"They haven't?"

"No!"

"Oh. Well," the nurse said, guiding her away from the
door, lowering her voice, until they were standing in the
bleak vastness of the hospital hallway, just outside a
different closed door. Beyond the door came otherworldly
moans. "Mr. Wrigdd has had what's commonly called a
nervous breakdown. A neighbor heard him from across the
walls and called the police. Apparently, he was unap-

proachable. Violent. Very bad indeed. The paramedics brought him here. They had to, um, restrain him. For his own protection. We gave him a sedative. He's been sleeping for a while now. You can go in if you like." Mary turned, but the nurse held her back by the sleeve. "As I said, we had to, um, restrain him. Just so you're prepared. Go on, honey. The poor boy."

She stood outside his door, her hand on the doorknob, heart pounding. She pushed on the door. With the door partly open there was barely enough light to make out the T.V. in the corner, the chair, and the bed. It was only after she was beside the bed that she could see him, flattened there with his legs and torso secured. She looked down at him in the dim light, and as her eyes adjusted she saw the wild hair, and new bruises to his face. His drugged eyes opened and closed stupidly like the mouth of a fish, his lips uttering faint, unintelligible nonsense.

She sat in the chair beside him, and took his hand. His hand closed tightly around hers, held on, then let go and did not close again. She touched the bruises, brushed the hair from his forehead, stroked his hair and cried silently. She looked upon him the way the captain of a great ship looks upon beached rubble which once was that great ship. The unconquerable had been conquered. What she had been denying, could now not be denied. The truth was before her, the devastation was complete. She turned her head and with her mouth buried in her sleeve, wept as she had never wept.

In the morning he awoke, and because he could not move he looked at the empty ceiling. He had no idea where he was. He thought he was dreaming. He felt pain on his face, and in his legs, and he wondered why he couldn't move. He thought that if you had a machete you could slash a checkers board on the ceiling and play with magnetic pieces, and then you wouldn't be bored. But because his arms and legs weren't functioning, he'd have to find another way to move the pieces. Maybe the flies could act as pieces for him. But the flies were all the same color. Even if he could coax them into helping, how would he be able to tell his own flies from the opponent's flies?

"You be red," he mumbled, his eyes opening and closing. "*You*, be red."

Mary, when she awoke, ran for the nurse. The nurse was not the one from the night before.

"He's shaking!" she cried out to the nurse.

"Who?" the nurse said, springing to her feet.

"My friend—Jerry Wrigdd!"

The nurse ran with her into the room. She checked his temperature, took his blood pressure, and then gave him another shot. Soon his body softened, and went limp. The nurse, younger than the others, offered to buy her a cup of coffee. They sat in the cafeteria where other doctors congregated in small groups, casually chatting. Friends and relatives of other patients sat one or two each to a table. Some you could tell were in rapture, while others had just seen first-hand the irreversible cruelty of fate. Between them shuffled a woman, an old woman, a tired woman, who pushed a cloth broom across the floor. The smell of bad coffee and disinfectant hung in the air.

"I was on duty yesterday morning when he came in,"

said the nurse. "You're Mary?"

"Yes," Mary said. "How do you know?"

"We found this in his pocket," she said and handed her the letter. The letter had been crumpled, but was now folded neatly. The nurse waited until she had read the letter.

"It doesn't seem to be a suicide note," the nurse reasoned, her body slumped heavy against the chair. "From what I can tell it's just a note to himself. It seems to be a love letter. But she's dead, isn't she, the woman in the letter? I've read about him in the papers. He's the one fighting the stadium. I've been following it."

"She died last fall."

"Has your friend been delusional before?"

"Delusional? I don't know what you mean."

"The letter, it almost seems as though she were alive. I know people write letters they don't send, but this one, I don't know. He must really believe he *can* travel through time," she said.

"And you don't?"

The nurse raised her eyebrows.

"They don't come packaged the way you all want them to, you know."

"Who?"

"Whoever it is you're waiting for."

"Waiting? I'm not waiting for anyone."

"Then whatever it is you believe in. It always announces itself in disturbing ways."

The nurse nodded, more of an acknowledgement than in agreement. Her hand massaged the thick paper cup. She watched the cleaning woman. She watched her coworkers at another table, who also watched the woman. Then she watched an older couple at a near table who grieved together, oblivious to any other thing in this world. She had not yet learned the art of complete detachment.

"He was talking to himself," she said. "Your friend. When he first came in, before he was drugged, he was talking to himself. Although he was agitated, he spoke in a calm manner. It's just that, well, the things he was saying, they don't make much sense to me. I thought they might to you." The nurse removed a napkin from her pocket. "I wrote these down last night, what I could remember. I couldn't sleep. I never have trouble sleeping, but last night I was up most of the night. I could leave this with you if you'd like," she said, pushing the napkin toward her.

Mary gazed at the napkin, reached for it, but then pushed it back. "Please, just read it to me."

"Sure," said the nurse. "Like I said, he wasn't making much sense. I'll just read what I wrote down." She laid the napkin on the table, flattened it with her palm, then picked it up by the top corners.

"Revolution. Revolution. Overcoming. The struggling. Overcoming. Broken backs, broken hearts. Overcoming. Overcoming. Bondage broken. Human suffering—ways around. Revolution. Mother England. Broken backs, reds and blacks. Overcoming. Overcoming. Struggle. Suffering. Overcoming. Poverty. Wars. Sorrow. Hopelessness. Human suffering. Overcoming. Overcoming. Overcoming. Broken backs, wounded hearts. Knowledge. Enlightenment. Knowledge. Enlightenment. Open hearts. Enlightenment. Overcoming. Overcoming. But knowledge misused.

Knowledge mismanaged. Knowledge turned against itself. Masters enslaved by knowledge of the ages. Obsolete purpose. Human triviality. Emptiness. Entropy. Boredom. Regurgitation. Human suffering. Arrogance. Ignorance. Pissing. Pissing. Pissing. Pissing!" The nurse hung her armpits on the back of her chair, still holding the napkin. "He kept saying that, over and over. What do you think?"

Mary held out her hand, the nurse gave her the napkin. She looked at it. She read the words. In reading them she heard him, clearly, and knew exactly what they meant.

"I don't know," she said, giving the napkin back.

The nurse took it, folded it neatly, and slipped it back into her pocket. "You don't have any ideas?"

Mary shook her head.

"Hmm," she sighed. "That's too bad. He's been under a lot of stress, the stadium and all. It's just strange. It wasn't like he was paranoid, or even frightened. He seemed to be watching something, something horrible, unable to do anything about it. That's it. It was like he was watching a disaster occur, and was unable to do a thing about it. I watched him. I watched him after he'd first fallen asleep."

"You watched him?" Mary asked, her eyes darting up as the nurse's darted down.

"His face moved. His eyes. His temple. His hands reached out, but could not find what they were reaching for. I've never seen eyes like those. What has he been through, I asked myself; where does he come from? He's not like the others that come in, is he?"

"The others? I wouldn't know about the others."

104

"He's not. He's a religious man?"

"Religious?"

"Why are you smiling?"

"He was an atheist once."

"An atheist," the nurse said. "I don't see it."

"No, I suppose not."

"Him?"

"You don't know who you have up there," Mary said.

The nurse brought the napkin close again and reread it. She looked up. "I don't understand. I just don't understand."

Vaguely, he remembered someone sitting beside him, the uncomfortable intrusion of metal into his arm, white figures coming and going from the room. The white figures made a habit of asking him if he felt like hitting anyone, or if he was feeling angry anymore, or if he'd had a violent father or uncle. They would whisper at the foot of the bed, check the straps which seemed to be slicing his flesh as though he were a bound roast, and then they'd leave. What could he have done? His thoughts quickly turned fatal. Did I *kill* someone, he thought to himself? Is that why I'm here?

The next morning one of the white figures came in, and he saw that she was a nurse. He was glad that she was a nurse because it meant he was in a hospital and not in jail, or in some worse place. The nurse checked his pulse and blood pressure. She opened the curtains and he was showered with light. She changed the water in the vase of flowers which sat on the table beside him. He lifted his head to see the nurse with her back turned, exploring the nooks of her ear with a finger, gazing out the window. She rubbed her fingers together. She checked the other ear the same as the first, and rubbed her fingers together. He brought his head back down. His head was heavy after not supporting it for days. Suddenly, a face loomed above his own. It was the face of the nurse. He was trapped beneath ruby lips and ruby teeth and auburn stalactites and excruciating breath. He let out a shriek. The face of the nurse jerked back, cackling. There was the squeaky, sticky sound of aerobic shoes fading from the room.

The next thing he knew he was hot and sweaty. He was running down a black corridor, running from something, but his feet seemed to be paralyzed. The drumming that was in the distance came closer. He tried to scream but couldn't. He knew that if he could scream, the dream would have to end. He summoned all his strength. He opened his eyes—something was clutching his arms—some giant bird clutching his arm—he saw a familiar face hovering above his own. He saw the sharp stalactites dangling inches from his eyes, the ruby piano teeth, the cavernous, flaming nostrils, the thousands of pores clogged with sweat and wax and pollution, gaping, inhabited with microscopic dinosaurs—also with flaming nostrils—moving with surprising agility for dinosaurs—up and down the mountains through the pore valleys. He thought he might fight back with breath of his own, so he let out his best fire-breathing effort in hopes of torching the thing.

"Jerry," it croaked.

He breathed harder.

"Jerry," it came again.

He concentrated on the eyes, hoping to blind it.

"Stop it. You're spitting all over yourself."

The thing carried a familiar disguise to its voice. After some time his eyes focused. The thing was not a thing at all. It was Mary.

He cried with joy. She wiped his mouth and chin. She hugged him, then wiped the tear trails from his face and sat across his chest so he could see her. Nothing ever felt as good as the weight of human friendship upon his chest.

"Can we go now?" he said.

She shook her head. "You've been a bad boy."

"How bad?"

"You don't remember?"

"Nothing."

"Mike Tyson's got nothing on this kid," she said.

"I didn't—"

"No," she said, "nothing too serious. You beat up your apartment pretty good."

"How long will I be here?"

"That depends on how well you fool the doctors into thinking you're normal."

"I'm finished," he said.

"Try and be a good domino for the next few days, will you?"

"What day is today?"

"Wednesday."

"How long have I been here?"

"Since Friday."

"Friday," he said to himself, thinking. "Do something for me. Tell me it was all a bad dream. Nothing but a bad dream."

"You mean the last five days?"

"No. Thursday and before."

"You know better," she said to him.

"I don't know anything."

"If you don't know anything, then our ship is sunk."

"Let it sink," he said.

"You're tired," she said, rubbing the end of his nose with her finger. "Every sailor needs some time ashore."

"And some like it so well, they never go back."

"And some never go back; but not your kind."

"Mary," he said, "I *am* tired."

"That's why you're here. You need rest."

"Don't," he said. "Please, don't."

"I have to. You're the only hope I've got."

"Hope?" he said. "Hope for what?"

"That things will change."

"Things will change. Of course they'll change."

"That's my boy," she said, rubbing his nose again.

"They'll change because fashions change, or a war will produce change, or fanaticism will sneak past the sleeping dogs of freedom; or an asteroid will change things, or the money will run out on all this and there will be change, the new Huns will rush in, and you bet there'll be change. But it won't come because of human need. It won't come from intellect, or kindness, or compassion. It will come on the untetherable wind, a seed caught by forces beyond its will or control. Oh, it will come. It may take one, two, three, four generations, but it will come, be assured. I'm sorry," he said dejectedly, "but I find no meaning in such a change.

There's no comfort in waiting for a wind which may or may not come in my lifetime. A wind so completely disassociated with humanity. There is no reason to believe."

"But, to no longer believe means to lose hope in mankind. *Jerry.*"

"Yes. Not mankind the species—*he* will always, somehow, hang around, stupidly, basely—but mankind the wise. Mankind the compassionate. Mankind the potential."

"But," she said, searching, "there's always hope. I'm here sitting beside you because of hope."

"Hope. What is hope but optimism, even minimal optimism, of the unknown? There is little of man's nature I don't know, and because of it little to be optimistic about. There is no reasonable basis for hope."

"But, Jerry," she said, pushing on his immoveable frame.

"I've been a fool for thinking there was anything more waiting behind that door. I thought, if only the door could be opened. Now I know. There is no door. It was a mirage. It was there because I wanted it to be there. There because I had this fear of it not being there. Fear doesn't make something real. I have an inability to deal with all this, so I invented a fantasy. It's been done before. I stood disbelieving as they failed to see my fantasy. It drove me crazy. All this time *they've* been the ones who've looked truth in the eyes. Who was I to expect more?"

"Who were you to expect more? You were the sole voice of perspective."

"A curse unless you can do something about it."

"You can."

"Look at me."

"I am looking at you."

"You're looking at a lunatic."

"I'm not listening to you," she said, covering her ears. "I can't hear you."

XIII

She took him home to her apartment. There she fed him,
read to him, and watched for signs of danger. She worked
her usual hours at the nursery. When she was gone, he sat
in the kitchen drinking coffee looking out the window at
the birds. He sprinkled birdseed on the back porch each
morning. He became familiar with them. He learned their
habits. He saw how the titmice came in groups of five to
eight, first with only one or two as sentinel, and then, once
the general feeding area had been deemed safe, the others
moved in, gradually pushing out the chickadees or even the
aggressive sparrows. The titmice weren't aggressive
themselves, but had numbers in their advantage. He liked
the blue jays, though they were mean and loud. He liked
the cardinals, whom he viewed as Athens to the blue jays
who were Sparta. He liked the juncos who were small and
plump and unfussy. He liked them all. He watched them for

hours. He sat at the table and looked out the window and watched them through sun, rain, or snow, come to the feeder and eat.

He slept on the couch downstairs. At times he would hear the faint creak of her bed as she shifted in sleep. It was why he could not sleep for at least an hour after going to bed. Waiting for the sound became like watching the birds. The birds were reason to get up, they occupied his days and filled his mind with curiosity, and amusement. The faint creak of her bed gave him reason to anticipate nighttime. After dinner each evening he waited for its approach. Sometimes he feigned weariness just so she would retire early. He wondered what she wore to bed. He pictured her as she lay in her bed, curled on her side, warm. The creak allowed his imagination to work. There was mystery in it.

After many nights his hearing became sharper, he was able to pick up sounds which before he had either ignored as insignificant, or had not heard at all. One of these sounds was an even fainter creak than the creak made by her shifting. It occurred regularly, constantly. In the beginning he did not notice it. But now he heard it almost as soon as he lay down. For many nights he heard it—it kept him lying awake nearly until dawn wondering, eliminating, conjuring. One morning he crept upstairs. Why should he be creeping up the stairs? Even he could not answer. But when his feet took him right instead of left to the bathroom, to the threshold of her room, a room which was not taboo in any way, a room in which they watched late movies regularly together on her bed, a room he was welcome to enter with or without her; when his feet took him over that threshold that morning, he trembled inside.

He walked about the room. It was like being among lost treasures suddenly discovered. He felt himself an imposition, disturbing these treasures from centuries of solitude. But they were not relics. They were of the here and now, their owner was alive, she was beautiful; these strewn brassieres, the crowded vanity, the dark sturdy trunk at the foot of the bed, the unmade bed itself, the shoes everywhere, were only days old in their current state.

He leaned against the bed. His eyes followed the elegant curves of the vanity. The legs were delicate, like spindles. They bowed outward, gracefully, to join the greater bulk of the vanity. The wood was dark, polished smooth from years of touching, brushing, dusting. The outer lines above where the wood molding encased three separate mirror panels, contrasted with the white plaster behind it, rendering the entire vanity body naked. Often they would be watching a movie and he would fall asleep. She would let him sleep. In the morning he would awaken to the sight of her, in a robe, or towel, or nothing, her back muscles flashing on and off like small fireflies, the line of her spine in a supple S, like a sapling, her hair cascading over her shoulders, and in the mirror the reflection of her face, always watching him, always *watchful* of him, her eyes heavy, in them the offer of more, the torturous patience of one in waiting. He rarely was affected by the sight of her. But now, now that she was gone, he was overwhelmed with her presence.

The poems were in a brown piece of pottery, a short, wide jug. He had seen them, sticking out of the jug, often before. He had thought about them, then tried not to think

113

of them, alternately, like any other temptation. He was not even certain they were the poems. That's what he told himself when he wanted to forget he could ever put words down on paper with clarity, and honesty, and beauty. It was easier believing he was never something he now was not. But there were times he couldn't help himself, and he gazed at the white, rolled pages sticking up from the jug while she combed her hair, or lined her lips sparingly with protective gloss, and he wondered why she had kept them, and if she ever went back and reread them, and if she did if they moved her. Hers were the unfinished ones. Those in progress, before he gave them to *her*. They were not written for her, or about her. He asked her for feedback, she gave it to him. They were friends. Never did he think, in his blind passion, what he was doing to her.

He took the jar, pulled all the poems out in a single handful, and laid them on the bed. He opened the first one, which rolled against his knee, and read it. The words returned him to the place of its origin, to its seed, to her. The moment passed through him, affected him, moved him as though he were reliving it. Something cracked open inside him. Something escaped from the crack and filled his being. Something gently shook him, and something awoke within him. He could not yet come to grasp it, to surround its meaning. It intuitively guided small corners of thought and emotion, yet it was familiar, and in the familiarity he found comfort, reassurance, and minute bits of confidence.

He read each poem carefully. Several times he decided to stop, to put them away, and once again forget about them. But he continued on. He wept for remembered moments of happiness. He wept for forgotten morsels of female love, affection, companionship. He wept for who he once was.

It was late in the afternoon when, exhausted, he lay back on her bed and found sleep. She came home and found him there. She closed the door and began to make dinner. When he awoke it was twilight. Snow moved past the window like tinsel. He smelled something wonderful, and heard the distant sound of humming. And then, he heard the sound. The sound which had brought him upstairs. The mystery sound. The regular, constant creak. He listened closely. He put two fingers to his wrist, pressed lightly. It was the pulse of his own heartbeat which creaked the bed.

XIV

She came down one morning and pushed on him with her foot.

"Get ub," she said, brushing her teeth.

"What?"

"Ged ub. Come on, we're leabing."

"Huh?"

"Ged *ub*," she said, poking her toes into his ribs.

"Aah!" he said, twisting away. "That tickles."

"Pag some clothes."

He pointed to her shirt. A drop of toothpaste was crawling down her front.

"Shid."

"Where are we going?" he said sitting up, hugging the pillow and blanket.

"Where are we goween, where are we *goween*?" she said mocking him, and went back upstairs.

They left two hours later. It was sunny, the streets were wet and noisy from melting snow. He put his hands in his pockets, leaned back, and sat silently as the city passed before them, and then was behind them and they were on the highway heading east. It had been a long time since he'd seen the countryside. From the highway things looked dirty and dead, and he wondered how anything could survive in winter. He saw hawks in the air and in the trees, dogs tied to chains trotting in circles in the mud, children sliding down hillsides three to a sled, and a woman standing on her stoop with arms crossed smoking a cigarette. He knew that winter could be an inconvenience, or a killer. It was a killer when you let your guard down and disrespected it as an inconvenience. That's when a storm or cold snap could get you.

The mountains were snowy and gusty. The highway was busy with eighteen-wheelers creeping uphill and then barreling down the other side. When they passed they dumped salt and muddy snow on the windshield. The muddy snow blinded them and the blast of air pressure moved the vehicle.

"I still have fantasies," he said.

"Do you?"

"One involves these trucks, and an F-14."

"That's nice," she said.

"I think so," he said reflectively.

The mounds of bare trees shimmered against the wind; the sky stretched wide to distant hills, and groups of hills, and whole new mountain ranges which were like the long and bulky frames of alligators compared to the turtle shells that were the hills. Across the mountains it was sunny again. The snow disappeared from the road, and then from the land. They passed through valleys with their fallow squares of gray, black, even green, delineating man from man, domesticated beast from domesticated beast, though not free beast from free beast. He looked into vehicles going past. Children waved at him, and he waved back. He noted license plates and wondered where everyone was going.

They stopped to get gas.

"You pump, I'll pay," she told him.

"Man," he said stepping from the car. "It's warm." He jumped in place with his rear sticking out and his arms bent in V's. As he stood pumping gas he watched her cleaning the windshield, and saw the other men looking at her, some leering at her, some offering smiling courtesy as she went inside and got in line to pay. An old man in a pickup pulled in on the other side of the pump. He got out of the pickup slowly, without expression of either pain or fatigue, which usually accompanies such slowness.

He finished pumping and got back in the car. He watched the old man. The old man wore overalls which blew in soft ripples, but the cloth did not show his form, so slight was the man. The old man rested his elbows on the truck, and rested his head on his thick fingertips. He wore a cap. Beneath the cap his neck lay naked to the sun. It was a neck like none he had ever seen. The neck was like that of a palm, composed of criss-crossing lines, except that these lines were far deeper. The lines were so deep, they functioned as joints. He wanted to feel the neck. He wanted to possess a neck like the old man's, but he knew a neck like his was scored from time itself, and even if he spent the rest of his days stooped over beneath the sun, he would never have a glorious neck like that. It was something earned, from a lifetime of physical labor beneath the sun. He thought, a neck like this old man's belongs in a museum, or shrine, or in books. In a museum, or shrine, or book, people would marvel at it and appreciate how it was acquired. They would honor the old man, instead of ignoring him.

It was then he noticed the old man looking at him in the reflection of the truck window. The old man was grinning at him, his mouth in the shape of a not so symmetrical oval. The old man said something. He rolled down the window to hear him, but just then Mary opened the car door and got in.

"What's the matter?" she said, handing him a cup of coffee.

"Nothing."

"Did you want something else instead?"

"No," he said. "It's nothing."

As she turned the ignition, the old man nodded, and then, as they were pulling out, he winked.

Turning from the highway, she took quiet, older roads she seemed to know by heart, for he never saw her look at a map. The soil turned red, bare hardwoods gave way to a mixture of hardwoods and pines. They passed vast farms, some with men working them and some not; some already with faint beads of green striping the soil. There were crumbling relics taken by vines, where no one lived now,

119

where people lived perhaps not too long ago.

He offered to drive, but she said she knew the way. He curled on his side and slept. He awoke to the smell of something pungent; an earthy pungency, familiar, and ripe, and sharp. For a moment he was lost in the smell, it seemed like a dream, but as his consciousness gained control of his mind, as memories sent signals of happier times to his brain, it came to him: the sea.

They passed over small bridges, over swamps and creeks which held moonlight in their dark surfaces, between arched forests. He leaned over and checked the gas gauge. It said a quarter tank. He didn't know if a quarter tank would get them to their destination, and he was afraid for some reason to ask; so he sat back and looked out the window and took in the smell and eerie darkness, and waited to see what unfolded next.

She pulled onto a road which he thought was a driveway until he saw the small county road sign. He watched the turbulent clouds of dust behind them in the mirror and fell into a half-sleep, his head bobbing to the ruts and bumps in the road.

He felt a tapping on his knee.

"You awake, Sleepy?" she said warmly to him.

"Hmm?" he said, and brought his bobbing head over.

"We're almost there," she said. Her face seemed like the faces of the children who waved at him in the cars.

She turned a final time into a wedge between the pine canopy. Young branches bent backward, slapped at the car, then snapped back together after they passed. He could see no road, only the faint wedge in the canopy. The way opened into a sandy, grassy clearing. As he opened the door he heard the low smacking of water.

They took their bags and walked through a short trail until they came to a marsh. In the moonlight the water glowed mysteriously. A rowboat was tied to a small, warped dock at the edge of the reeds. Across the marsh, on a small island, sat a house.

"There it is," she said.

"There what is?"

"The house."

They rowed across to the island. There was a soothing, sweet-smelling breeze that moved over the water.

It was late and they were tired. She showed him around, briefly, and then they took their bags upstairs and got ready for bed. There were four bedrooms. She took hers, the one she had slept in since childhood, and then showed him to her parents' room at the end of the hall.

"Can't I have that room?" he asked, nodding back to her brother's room.

"Sure," she said, "but my parents' room is nicer. They have a better mattress."

"I know. But, your *parents'* room."

"Understood," she said, and did an about face. "I'm going to make up my bed. I'll be over to do yours when I'm finished."

"Mary, I can do it."

"Don't be silly," she said, patting his head as she left the room.

He laid back on the bare mattress and fell asleep. She gently roused him and led him to her bed. She helped him undress, and he slipped beneath the covers. He was vaguely aware of what was happening. He woke in the middle of the night wondering where he was. He chuckled out loud at the mystery until he noticed her slumbering figure on a bed across the hall, and he remembered. He lay back down. A familiar restlessness overtook him and denied him sleep for several hours.

She found him in the morning sitting on the longer of two docks, wrapped in a blanket, staring out at the water. The sun was up, but the sky was gray. He watched as a group of white birds danced together above the marsh, came to rest in shallow waters near shore, then stalked fish there on long, sharp legs.

"Morning," she said, rubbing the top of his head.

"Good morning," he said, turning from the birds to look at her.

"What are you reading there?"

He lifted the book from his lap. "Birds of the East Coast," he said.

"Did you sleep all right?"

"Like a baby."

"I like to sit here too. I can watch the birds for hours. I don't use the book much. I have my own names for them," she shrugged. "I just like to watch them. I'll squint my eyes and see their colors moving, and sometimes that's better than anything you could get from the book."

"You never mentioned this place," he said.

"I haven't been here for a long time. We used to come here for the summers. Mom and us kids would stay all summer. Dad would drive down every other weekend. Gosh, it was fun. You forget, until you come back."

"Do your brother and sisters come here?"

"Not much," she said. "Everybody's busy with families and careers. Well, except me. I don't have a career, I have a job. And I don't have a family, I have plants."

"That's a family."

"Yeah, I know."

"I have books and spiders," he said. "That's a family."

"I know."

"Maybe it is, maybe it isn't," he said philosophically.

"You want some?" she said, sitting down beside him, lifting her mug.

"Thanks," he said, and he took the mug and wrapped his hands around it and let his face feel the steam, before sipping from it.

"I had trouble sleeping," she said after a yawn.

"I had the better mattress."

"Yeah, maybe that's it."

"You didn't have to sleep there, you know."

"I didn't mind. I hardly ever have trouble sleeping," she said.

"We can switch tonight," he said, giving her back the mug. When he handed the mug back to her, their hands touched. Their hands had touched countless times before, under countless circumstances. It felt to him as though a feather were being traced along his fingers. She lowered her eyes. He rubbed his hands up and down his legs. "It's still winter," he said. "The water is cold."

"Do you still think of her?" she asked without looking

up.

"Do I still think of who?"

She waited, and then said, "Because it's all right if you do. It's perfectly natural. I was just wondering."

He looked at her, but she would not look up. He gazed out over the marsh which was never without movement or interest. The question no longer pierced him. For the first time it was merely a difficult thing to answer.

"I do," he said. "I think of her every hour of every day. Have you ever lost someone?"

She shook her head no.

"I'm glad," he said, and laid his hand upon her knee. He left it there. Softly, he caressed her knee. "It's hard to explain."

"You don't have to explain it—"

"But I want to," he said. "I think I need to."

"You don't *have* to—"

"Mary," he said, "just listen." His hand moved against her leg, and with each gentle stroke a new barrier was penetrated, and a new fledgling took flight. "When you lose someone, it's only your loss of memory that saves you. At least that's what I'm finding out. You forget what that person looked like in the detail you once knew, what they sounded like, what they felt like. Your memories aren't from that morning, or yesterday, they're from weeks, and then months ago. The spaces in your life once reserved for and occupied by that person, wait for new events, new memories, but of course they don't come. You wait and wait, but they don't come. Then these spaces, because your life does go on physically, if not willingly, become occupied by new events and memories, and they have nothing to do with the person you've lost. Sometimes you fight it. You feel like you're betraying their memory. You feel guilty. You feel as though you should never love again. Especially if you loved intensely and completely. Each day new memories are being put into the spaces, and old ones are fading. That's what saves you. You don't stop loving, you stop remembering. When you do remember, the pain is unbearable. If you want to survive, you condition yourself to forget.

"I could sit here and tell you that I don't think of her, that I've stopped loving her, but that would be a lie. I'm trying to look ahead, because that's where life is lived. If I had already forgotten her, what would you think of me?"

"She allowed you to travel. She wasn't just another woman. She was someone no one else could ever be."

"Maybe," he said, lifting his chin, looking to the sky. "I don't know."

"I do," she said. "How could I blame you for being someone I would die to be with; how could I want you to be less than that? Because I. . ."

"Because you what?"

"Nothing."

"Say it," he said, looking down at his hands.

"I have to do the dishes," she said, and got up. He caught her leg.

"Mary."

"Please let me go."

"What if I told you I couldn't say what you can't say? What if I told you I'm lost in the currents, but that they're

125

moving me farther along; that I want to say something, but I'm afraid; I don't want to feel what I've been feeling for the past six months ever again; I'm still sick, but getting better; I'm waking up, I just need time?"

"You can't say it for one reason. I can't say it for a reason altogether different. Don't say anything else."

She broke free from his hand and hurried toward the house. He turned, made a move to get up, but then stopped. He watched her run up the path to the house and disappear around the far side.

Some nights were warm, and she opened the windows and let the breeze fill the house. Other nights reminded them that winter would not give up easily. It was one such night, she was by the fire painting her toenails, while he sat in the old rocker, reading. She wore a pink flannel nightgown. Her hair sprawled in casual folds about her nape and shoulders. She hummed as she carefully took the small brush, dipped it in the clear bottle, and stroked her tiny nails. The fire flashed and popped. The light showed her form in shadows and straining flannel.

"How has the fishing been?" she said absently.

"Fishing?" he said, looking up from his book.

"Fishing. You've been taking the boat out. Are you catching anything?"

"Oh, the boat," he said. "I haven't been fishing."

"You haven't been fishing?" she said, grinning curiously. "Then what have you been doing out there?"

"Rowing."

"I know *rowing*. But where do you go? What do you do?

You're gone for hours."

"I get myself lost in the maze," he said.

"That's easy to do."

"I know it's easy to do. I'm an expert at it."

"Have you really been lost? I can show you around. I get lost sometimes myself."

"I get lost every day," he said. "But each day I get less lost."

She turned and gave him a look. "Are you talking about the marsh?"

"Of course I'm talking about the marsh. What else would I be talking about?"

"I don't know," she said, turning back around, focusing her attention on a square middle toe. "Sometimes I don't know what you're talking about. I think you're just playing with me."

"If I play with you, you'll know it. I promise—I'm not playing with you now. I go out each morning in the boat, and get lost. I enjoy getting lost. I try to get lost. I hope to get lost. And then I find my way back. It's doing wonders for my confidence, and my brain loves the exercise."

"You're silly," she smiled. When she smiled her cheeks balled up red and smooth, and it did something to him. He was doing very little reading. "Don't you think it's pretty out there?"

"It's beautiful," he said. "There's so much life. It's dizzying, like wine."

"My dad would think you're weird for not fishing."

"He wouldn't be the first."

"Don't you like to?"

"Sure, I like to."

"Then why don't you?"

"I don't have a license."

"You don't need one."

"I don't have a pole."

"There must be a dozen poles in this place, and you've tripped over half of them."

"I can't remember how to tie a knot."

"Why are you lying?"

"It comes naturally. And because I don't know how to present the truth."

"Jerry," she said, cocking her head, looking at her array of shiny toes. She moved them rhythmically. "Why can't you just say what you're thinking? You're always thinking. I know you are. So just open your mouth and say it."

"I'm involved in a secret society, and I can't tell anyone about it," he said matter-of-factly. "I can't even tell you."

"See. Wasn't that easy?"

"Very."

"Jerry."

"Yes."

"Tell me what you're thinking right now."

"I'm thinking, you look nice in pink flannel."

"That's not what you're thinking," she laughed. She looked back at him, then turned around and covered her mouth and laughed again.

"That's what I was thinking," he said. "See why I normally lie."

"Don't look at me anymore."

"What do you mean, don't look at you anymore?" he

said, pushing on her shoulder with his foot. "It's a free country."

She took a swipe at his foot with her arm. "Stop it. No, it's not a free country. Read your book."

"I was reading my book, until you started bothering me." He pushed on her shoulder again. She took another blind swipe at his foot. He pushed again.

"You're a real pest," she said.

"Okay, I'll stop."

She put both feet out in front of her. One was done, the other wasn't. He waited until she had forgotten, and then pushed on her shoulder again. Surprisingly, she didn't turn on him, as he wanted her to do. She scooted back against the rocking chair, took his leg beneath her arm, and began to paint his toes.

"Hey," he said.

"That's what you get. What's your favorite color?"

"Green."

"Ha-ha."

"It is."

"Why is it?" she asked.

"Because it's the color of life."

"Plant life. Not animal life. What's the color of animal life?"

"I don't know. Red maybe. That's the color of flesh, and blood."

"What's your favorite food?"

"Milk."

"That's not a food."

"What do you mean, it's not a food?"

129

"That's a drink. Why are you so difficult," she sighed. "Come on."

"Well," he said, taking time to think it over, "if you won't let me say milk, which is my first answer, then. . . I'll. . . have. . . to. . . say. . . spaghetti!"

"What's your favorite movie?"

"That's easy, *The Adventures of Robin Hood.*"

"You told me once it was *The Sound of Music.*"

"*The Sound of Music?* What kind of fairy do you think I am?"

She giggled. "I don't know, but I remember. It was a couple years ago. We were all out somewhere."

"I never said that."

"Yes, you did."

"Well, so what if I did?"

"I'm not the one making a big deal out of it."

"No, but it's your tone. It's all in the tone," he said, shaking his finger at her.

"Who do you think is the most beautiful woman in the world?" she said. Finished painting the toes on his right foot, she blew on them.

"You," he said sincerely, and without hesitation.

She was beating on a rug with a broom one afternoon when she saw the small boat coming in. He let go of the oars and waved. She pumped the broom in the air. He came marching up from the dock, his head lowered, eyes half-crazed.

"Oh yeah? What's up with you?" she asked, leaning on the broom.

"Hey, Edith. What's for dinner?" he said, but kept

walking.

She followed him around the corner of the house to the porch where he sat removing his rubber boots. She stared at him, broom still in hand, waiting for him to say something.

"You're not going to hit me with that, are you?" he said, giggling.

"Come on," she said. "Tell me."

"Oh, nothing."

"I *will* whack you with this," she warned, raising the broom.

"But it's nothing. Now go get me some gruel like a good wench."

She bopped him on the head.

"Ow."

"Wench yourself," she said.

"I'm a happy guy," he said. "What can I say?"

She narrowed her eyes suspiciously, then leaned closer and sniffed the air around his mouth. He laughed out loud.

"No," he said.

"Ah, well," she said, bopping him on the head once more for good measure, and went back outside to the rug. He took his time removing his boots. He had them untied, but then sat there staring down at them without moving, only listening. He waited until he heard the sound of the broom beating the rug.

He checked behind him, closing his body, and slipped a hand into his pocket. He wiggled his hand back out and opened it. There, in the very center of his palm, shining dully in the shade of the porch, was a coin. He marveled at it. He moved his palm this way and that, watching the shadows dig into the relief of the worn figure, making it come alive. He read the inscriptions on the coin, whispering in low, secretive murmurs. He had never been given a Walking Liberty for change before today.

He took the boat out into the folds of the marsh in the mornings, and then came in for lunch. In time, he began staying out through lunch, well into the afternoon, sometimes not coming in until nearly suppertime. There were fishing poles on the porch, but he never took them. He did take the small casting net. The casting net stayed with him at all times whenever he took the boat out. He'd drape it lovingly across the boat when he got back, to dry, and the next morning he'd gather it together and put it in the front part of the boat and shove off. He attended to his net as if it were his hunting dog.

In the evenings they sat on the porch. The mosquitoes weren't out yet. She said they weren't a problem for another two months, and then you couldn't sit on the porch without a lot of discomfort. Some nights they sat on the rocking chairs inside and made noise rocking on the wooden floor. Other nights they sat on the dock and watched for fish who jumped sideways in the air and came back down with a smack; at the same time they watched for the birds, gazed at the clouds, the moon and stars, the trees bending against salt breezes.

He took her out into the marsh. Already he knew his way around. He knew where certain birds lived, their habits, their calls, their appetites, their enemies, their advantages and disadvantages in flight. He knew the tiny shellfish who clung to reeds and rocks, he knew when the tides came and how the birds used them. When they went out they saw otters, turtles, raccoons, opossums, and snakes which swam both on the surface of the water and also below. There were no crabs yet. She explained how they were buried in the mud for the winter, and wouldn't be coming out until warmer waters returned.

"So what's the word?" she said one evening as they were rocking slowly in the big chairs.

"What do you mean?" he said.

"How's the book?"

He stopped rocking and held it up. "Same one. Birds of the East Coast."

"You have them all memorized by now?"

"Hardly," he said. "I have a real bad memory."

"So, what do you catch when you're out in your boat?"

"What do I catch?"

"Yeah, what do you catch?"

"I don't catch much of anything," he said.

"How's the net working out?"

"Can't seem to get the hang of it. Can't get it in a good circle."

"Yeah, it takes a while."

"Mostly, I just practice, if I use it at all."

"I see you laying it out to dry when you come in. You seem to take good care of it."

"Got that from my dad."

"Yeah, well, you seem to take awfully good care of it for not using it much."

"Like I said, thank the old man."

"You should take the fishing poles with you."

"Not a fisherman," he said. "Remember?"

"You'd catch all kinds of fish back in there."

"Really?"

"Oh, sure."

"Don't have any bait."

"There are plenty of lures in the tackle box. You should try it."

"Maybe some time."

"I know how to fry them up."

"Yeah, okay, well maybe one of these days."

"You get a bath yet?" she said, dropping her book on the floor, standing up.

"Not yet," he answered.

"I'm going up. You want to wash my back?"

He looked up from his book.

"Don't you want to?"

"Sure, I'll wash your back," he said.

"You don't have to."

"I said I will."

"Give me five minutes."

"Five minutes. Sure. I'll be up in five minutes."

He rocked more slowly in the chair, with his hands on his knees, until he thought five minutes had passed. He tried to think of a bird, or the marsh grass blowing in waves, but his eyes wandered to her rocking chair and the last image of her turning back to gaze at him as she went up the stairs. He heard the sound of the water, and that killed any chance for the birds or marsh grass. He waited another two minutes. Finally, he stood up. He wanted to put on his rubber boots and go out in the boat. Maybe he could call up to her. Maybe. . .

He pushed on the bathroom door, it gave way easily and without much noise. Through the billowing steam she appeared. Her hair was up in a loose knot, she rubbed at her neck with a sponge. He kneeled beside her. Stray strands of hair stuck flat against her neck. A few shorter curled hairs at the base of her neck were neither bound to the knot, nor caught by water against her skin, and stood aloft. There was only one sponge, so he waited.

She lathered the sponge, washed her arms, scrubbing lightly, then rinsed them after dipping the sponge in the water. She washed her chest and stomach. She moved back in the tub and washed her legs which were long and smooth and pink from recent sun.

"Do you think my legs are fat?" she said.

He knocked on her head. "Hello in there."

"I think they're flabby."

"I think you're crazy."

"Do you like them?"

"Your legs? Sure, I do. You have pretty legs."

"What do you like about them?"

"I don't know," he said, his eyes wandering from her legs to other places, then back again. "They're just pretty."

"Is that all you can say, 'They're just pretty'?"

"No."

"Well, what else?"

"They're not flabby, that's for sure," he said.

"Thanks a lot."

"They're not hairy like mine."

"You can stop now."

"No warts or rashes. No ringworm. Your cellulite count is low. Yup. Right pretty legs."

"How about the rest of me?"

"The rest of you. . ."

"Do you think I'm pretty, besides my legs?"

"You're beautiful," he said, unable to look into her eyes. "You know that."

"What part of me is beautiful?"

"Every part."

She stood up. The water gushed from her body and the tub swirled violently.

"Take a good look at me," she said, staring at the wall, trying to breathe normally. She turned slowly for his eyes. She looked at the tiles, some of which were cracked. She wondered if he knew how to fix them. The showerhead was leaky. She wondered if he could stop it from leaking. She wondered these things as his eyes moved over her nude figure. She wondered if he would spend the whole trip reading Birds of the East Coast. She wondered what he was seeing right now. Her breathing grew deeper. He surely noticed her rising and falling breasts. She wondered, what was he thinking. What was he going to do. What would she do.

He looked at her, then looked past her to the wall, then at her, then at the soap in the soap dish, then again at her form and things rumbled inside him; abstract, primitive images flashed before his eyes. The images grappled with his conscious self. For the first time since he could remember, he felt something for a woman, and was helpless to do anything to stop it.

"What are you thinking?" she said.

"I'm not thinking at all," he answered.

She stepped from the bath and as she did he held her hand and steadied her. He felt the warmth of her body, so close. Her eyes looked up into his. He wrapped his arms around her, put his chin on her shoulder, and held on.

They lay down on her bed. There was a warm breeze coming in through the window. He caressed her gently. She pushed herself toward him, and offered her lips.

XV

When the days were warm they rowed to a beach a half-mile south of the house. They sat on the beach, ran along the water's edge and shrieked at the cold. She ran from him, he would catch her, panting, sweating, and wrestle her to the sand where he could not go more than a few seconds without pressing her body against him, and moving against her, and kissing her brown skin.

She abandoned herself to this ripened fruit. She had experienced some semblance of love once before, but nothing so powerful as this. She had silently loved this man when he was loving *her*, giving her sleepless nights, prompting her to try different men, substitute men, and then after souring on the results of that, she closed in and forgot about love, only remembering it as some mysterious, miraculous nectar of life in some other place for some other people. For some things it is the anticipation itself which is the real sweetness. The actualization is anti-climactic, a letdown after the long, arduous assault against odds, self, or reason. But not this. This actualization bubbled over the cup of anticipation, spilling down the tall and sturdy ramparts of feminine grit, drenching her in its sublime bliss. Beneath his weight, his warmth, his smell, his sweat, she became someone else. This transformation went far beyond the primitive urges which prompted her hands, legs, eyes, lips, and voice to leap beyond their normal bounds; it was more than a lid opened, or hunger presented with nourishment. These interludes created paths of thought which could not have existed before his touch to her ear, back of her neck, breasts, inner thigh. They created colors unknown before his lips pressed hot flesh below her chin, beneath her calf, between the halves of her buttocks. He kneaded her flesh, and she was re-created from the bound, packaged person of her sex, was nudged aloft to float above the familiar patchwork of orderly sustenance, blossomed into unthinkable bursts of momentary clarity, wisdom, and time experience. She crashed through the barriers of current genius, obliterated the imaginable of the sages and proph-ets, uprooted long-held beliefs. It was not the physical act of love which did these things to her, but the immersion into love, the acceptance of it as guide and teacher. The act was but the trumpet sound to the lung power deep within, the effect—and what an effect it was—to a cause which could not be measured by any device. The cause, the *source*, was without definability. It fluttered outside the realm of human purpose—though how it pushed this purpose to its will. It would not unfurl for the rote worshipping, though her heart worshipped its design and her sensations worshipped its chosen method of expression.

"I love you," she said while lying atop his heaving chest. She bent and kissed him, using not only her lips, but hands, nails, teeth, and four limbs. "I do, I do, I do. . ."

They rolled across the sand. He picked her up, ran with her, set her gently down again. He grew fatigued, but the fatigue served only to make him giddy, and clumsy in his lovemaking.

"Jerry," she said now lying beside him. She reached out and touched his face. "Jerry," she repeated. His eyes seemed unburdened. His smile was easy and unforced. "Jerry," she said, stroking the side of his face, and she became teary-eyed, and her hand trembled.

Now when he came back from the marsh he sought her out, and held her and kissed her and could not get enough of her, and often she dropped a broom, or pan, or book, and he dropped his net, and they fell to the floor, or table, or couch, or sand. While in the boat he would think of her. He gazed into the water and saw her image, he watched a flock of birds and saw her dress flapping briskly in the wind, he tilted his head to the sun and knew that she was beneath the same sun. When they sat on the porch, she was on his lap, or their hands were playing across the space between the chairs. When they ate, their feet touched, they kissed between bites, she blushed beneath his gaze. In the evenings, while they were reading, tenderness floated through the silence and warmed them and prompted them to pause and reflect, or to gaze up.

The night was for whispers, and gentle touches. They

lay on her bed facing one another, the room illuminated by
moonlight or not, the air warmed by a breeze or the windows closed against a chill, and the eternal slow dance
between man and woman went on, and on, until drunken
bliss tugged at their eye lids and they fell asleep entangled
in each other's limbs.

One day he came walking up from the boat with his high-
shouldered, head-down gait of his, and before when he
would have said, "Hey, Edith, what's for dinner?" jokingly,
maintaining the proper distance between them with sar-
casm, he instead stopped, picked her up, twirled her around
so that her dress opened like an umbrella, and kissed her.
"Hello, sweetheart," he said. "Got anything to eat for a
hungry old fisherman?"

"I do," she said, "but you don't fish. Remember?"

"Oh, yeah," he said. "I've got to get cleaned up. Just
want to spray off outside. Be five minutes."

"I'll be right in," she told him. That's what she said. But
when she went to turn toward the house, to follow his
footsteps to the outdoor shower, she turned instead toward
the marsh and the small boat. She began walking toward
the dock, without any special curiosity or suspicion, or
even later looking back on it, premonition. She found
herself standing on the dock looking out over the dark
waters, smelling the air, smiling beneath the sun. She had
no reason to look down into the boat, but she did look
down into it, and there beside one of the oars lay a spear.

She got in the boat and picked it up. It was long and
very slim, made entirely of wood. It had a red point. She

dipped the point of the spear into the water, the water clouded, and she knew it was blood. She threw it against the side of the boat and went to step out when her foot kicked something firm, but not hard. Something lay beneath the net, which was not stretched neatly across the boat to dry, but was bunched together in a tangle. She pulled at the bunched netting—then let out a cry. For there, in the bottom of the boat, lay the very large head of a fish.

She was standing on the dock looking down into the boat when he came hurrying down.

"Jerry," she said, "there's a fish head in your boat."

"Beauty, ain't she?" he answered nervously, shifting his weight from foot to foot, hands in his back pockets.

"But you don't fish."

"See, normally I don't, that's the funny thing."

"So what made you decide to fish today?" She turned toward him and waited for an answer.

"What made me decide to fish today," he stalled. "Hmm. . . you know, I'm not sure."

"The mood just struck you?"

"Yeah, you could say that."

"With this spear?"

"What spear?"

"That spear," she said, pointing.

"*That* spear. Oh."

"Where did you get it?"

"That spear?"

"Jerry."

"Right," he said scratching his head. "Where did I get the spear."

"You didn't make it yourself?"

"No, I didn't," he said.

"You found it."

"No, I didn't find it," he said.

"Someone gave it to you."

"That's right," he said moving his hands from his back pockets to his hips. "How'd you guess?"

"Who gave you the spear?"

"A man."

"What man?"

"A man. He lives—" he nodded toward the marsh "—out there."

"What's this man's name?"

"Funny thing about that," he said scratching his head again, "but I can't get it right. It's sort of hard to pronounce. I just call him Big Hands. You should see them, his hands I mean. My gosh. And strong!"

"Has he lived here long?"

"Oh, yes."

"Then tell me his name. I should know it."

He turned away, mumbling.

"What was that?"

"Oh, you wouldn't know him, I don't think. Hmm. . . I don't think so, no. . ."

"Jerry?" she said, pulling his arm, and in doing so bringing the rest of him back toward her.

"He's an Indian."

"An Indian? I don't know of any Indians around here."

"They don't come out much," he said. "Only for me."

"Is that who gave you the chains and shackles?"

143

He mumbled again, drifting away.

"Jerry Wrigdd, you come back here," she said.

He drifted back. "Oh. Those. . . you found them. . ."

"I saw them behind the shed. Chains and shackles are the kinds of things you tend to notice lying around, especially when we've never had any on the island before."

"Can you imagine," he said, trying to shift focus, "wearing those."

"Where did you get them?"

"From a girl," he mumbled, lowering his head. "A girl, that's right. A fifteen-year-old girl. I broke them off her ankles." He looked up. "A fifteen-year-old girl wore those around her ankles, Mary."

"And this girl, where does she live?"

"Same place," he nodded, "out there."

"In the marsh."

"In the marsh. But now," he said smiling, "now her feet are free! *Free.* We can only imagine that kind of freedom."

"Jerry," she said, making him look at her. "Are you travelling again?"

"No," he said. "I don't know how, or why exactly, but now they're coming to *me.*"

"Who's coming to you?"

"People," he said.

"The people in your travels?"

"Many of them are, but many of them I've never met before. The girl, I never met her before. Big Hands, I knew his village, but not him. He was a boy when I spent time in his village. The woman at the diner, I'd forgotten her, but I remembered when I saw her again. The man at the gas station who's been following us; I'd never met him before."

"What man at the gas station?"

"The old man with the beautiful neck. He was getting gas the same time as us on the way down. You probably didn't notice."

"I don't remember an old man at any gas station," she said trying to recall.

"Yeah, like I said, apparently he followed us down here. He's living in a tent—"

"In the marsh."

"That's right," he said.

She shook her head. "I don't know who you're talking about."

"It doesn't matter."

"So, they're coming to you?"

"They are."

"What do they want?"

"I don't know what they want from me, but I can tell you what they want in general. The same thing they've always wanted. They want to be heard."

"By who?"

"By anybody, for starters. They know me, they know I'll listen. They know I take them seriously. They know I respect them. But having one of your own listen doesn't get you very far if nobody else is listening, and it won't be enough."

"I don't understand. What do you mean, it won't be enough?"

"I mean there comes a time when ignorance is no excuse. Their time has passed, they know that, but the road ahead is long and still undetermined. They care about it. It's been laid by their backs, and they want to have a say."

"You sound serious."

"Mary," he said, taking her by the arms, "for the first time they have a voice. And not just a voice, but an avenue to real power!"

"You," she said.

He shoved his hands in his front pockets. "I guess so."

"But, you don't care."

He wandered to the corner of the dock. "It makes no sense," he said. "I don't want to care. I remember where caring got me before. But, I wake up each morning and row out into the marsh, and there I meet them. I listen to their stories, see their needs, and there's nothing to intellectualize. I either help, or I don't help. For me, I can't not help. It's like trying not to breathe or eat. I'm no different from those who can't help themselves, and prey on humanity. It's in their blood, as the opposite is in mine. There's nothing to praise or condemn here, because it's beyond free will."

She stood close to him. "What do they want you to do?"

"I don't know," he said. "I honestly don't know."

In the morning he came down to the boat and found her sitting on the dock. She said she wanted to go with him. She wanted to see these people, she wanted to talk to them, hear their stories, and learn from them. He said that was fine by him, but he couldn't guarantee anything. They were wary of people and as far as he knew trusted only him.

They got in the boat. He pushed it away from the dock,

and then dropped the oars into the water. He rowed nearly to the point, and then took a branch north which opened up like a pond. Its banks were steep and muddy on one side, and grassy on the other. He rowed through the middle of the pond. The boat cut through the water, ripples moved slowly away from it and gave quick thrills to a group of ducks and a pelican. She felt happy. She sat in front and closed her eyes, or held them open, and when they were open she pointed the way. She leaned over the bow and spread her arms and touched the water and looked at her own reflection.

"How far do you usually go?" she called back.

"Oh, it depends. Some days this is as far as I go. Other days I go deep into the swamps."

"How far are we going today?"

"We've got a ways to go yet."

"Have you seen anybody?"

"No. Haven't seen anybody."

"Should we get out and look for them?"

"We'll get out near the village," he said.

"Where Big Hands lives?"

He nodded, then yelled back, "Yeah!"

He took a stream which wound back and forth, split several times, and was joined several more times by other streams. He brought them alongshore beneath some low, thick branches. She had packed sandwiches. They ate beneath the trees.

"Are you frightened of something?" she said.

"Why do you say that?"

"You seem worried."

147

"Do I?"

"Are you thinking of, you know?"

"Back home? Maybe," he said. "But it's not that I'm worried about what will happen to me. I'm worried about *them*."

"Who?"

"All of them."

"The people of Cowopolis? They hate you."

"Let them hate me. They can hate me all they want. I don't care; they're ignorant. Ignorance needs to be cured, not condemned. It's the toughest illness to cure, because its symptoms are invisible to the afflicted. How do you convince a people that they're all sick? It's the challenge of challenges, the challenge that repeats itself regularly in the march of generations."

She wanted to hold him and press his chest against hers and feel his heartbeat. "Jerry, where did you come from?"

"Not *you*," he said grinning.

"You're not human. Were you taught to feel as you do, or were you born with it? You couldn't have learned it. No one could learn something like that. And if you were born with it, then you really aren't human because no human alive cares so little about himself and feels so much for others. You do know why they hate you? They hate you because you demand from them effort, introspection, doubt; when the whole set-up is geared for ease, for auto-mated, thoughtless living. The rules they live by don't allow for a Jerry Wrigdd."

"Some of their rules do," he said.

"Not many."

"No, not many," he agreed.

"I think deep down they realize what's become of us. But in the downward spiral it's impossible for them to escape. It's now habit. It's in their mores, they teach it to their children. You're forcing them to question not a stadium, but the fruition of three hundred years. You must know they'll not do it willingly."

"They will see, Mary," he told her. "They will."

They pushed on, moving deeper into the maze. It felt good having the crisp, sudden breezes in their faces. She closed her eyes and thought of recent lovemaking. She thought of his kisses beginning at her neck, and travelling down. She thought of this same thing over and over.

The boat bumped land. Here a trail led them up and over a small crest, and across an open, sandy plateau. He stopped several times to show her what he said were footprints in the sand. It was plain to see how at home he was in the marshland, and plain to see why he struggled in the other place. They came upon a stand of pines, and here the path seemed to vanish. Without hesitation, he took them through the trees and out the other side to another clearing. He stopped.

"What is it?" she said.

He put his hands on his hips, looked out over the clearing, back to the stand of trees, then back to the clearing. He shook his head.

"Jerry?"

"They couldn't have," he said.

"Is this where you thought we'd find them?"

"It's gone."

She was afraid to say anything.

"The village. It's not here. It was, but now it's gone."

He showed her the exact spot. They stood where the dwellings stood, but the grass was not matted down or worn. It was as natural as any grass unaffected by human contact. There were no fire spots, or holes where posts had been sunk into the sand. There was no evidence of the dogs, or horses. No fragments of leather, pottery, woven baskets, or waste.

She stayed close, following his eyes, and then his long strides across areas which could not have been recently vacated by people. She remained silent. He became frantic, then pensive, then numb. He stood without moving, staring into the sand.

"Are you sure it was *here*? Maybe, you know. . ."

"Positive," he said.

"Let's sit down," she offered. "Try and remember."

"I can't believe it. It was here. They've gone back."

"Maybe we took a wrong turn," she said.

"No. They're not here anymore." He fell to his knees, his face contorted, his body shaking. "I don't understand." He knew it was the spot. He came here nearly every day. There was no mistaking it. He panicked. What if they all were gone, never to come back, with no way of reaching them? He took off running.

They travelled upstream and he looked for them, but found nothing. There was no trace of them ever being there. Finally as night approached he rowed back toward the house, dejected and confused. As he brought the boat alongside the dock, and as he lifted the oars from the water and tucked them in the boat, he could not raise his eyes. He waited for her to go first, muttered something about having to spread the net out to dry, and sat without moving until it was dark. She was sitting on the porch steps when he came up. "Do you believe me?" he said to her. "That's all I want to know."

She looked at him. She had been crying. "How can I not believe you?" she replied.

"They're gone," he said in a deflated voice as he trudged up the porch steps and opened the screen door. "They're gone."

Each morning he went out as before, but came back having seen no one, except now that winter was finally dying a few fishermen with their fast boats and narrow purpose. He returned disappointed, but not broken, and as the days wore on even the disappointment faded and he went into the marsh expecting only to see birds and fishes and turtles, and though he hadn't forgotten, he no longer waited.

She stayed beside him more often. He took her with him in the boat, instead of going alone. The crabs were back and they began catching them with strings and chicken necks. Mostly he liked to just look at them as they nervously snapped at his fingers. They'd stop in the middle of the marsh and toss out two or three lines, wait for them to become taut, and then slowly pull them in. When the crabs weren't hitting, they talked, or gazed into each other's eyes, or he pulled up her tank top and lost himself in her warmth and softness, and often they made love in the boat. In the

151

mornings he woke and studied her face, and form. He watched as sunlight moved across the room, changing the shadows that her nose, eyebrows, lips, shoulders, breasts, made upon other parts of her, or on the bed covers, or on him. He watched her sigh contentedly, and he wondered what she was dreaming. He stroked her skin, and spoke to her. He forgot about the boat and crabbing and everything else, and watched her until she woke, her big green eyes opening, her back arching, arms stretching, and then he touched her tenderly.

"How long can we stay?" he asked her.

"Until the money runs out," she said.

"What about your job?"

"What about it?"

"Do you still have one?"

She laughed. "I don't know. I told Mike I'd be gone for two weeks."

"Maybe you should call them."

"I know."

"I'm sorry," he said.

"Don't be silly."

"Do you want to go out today?"

"Not if it means leaving this."

"Is that a 'no'?"

"That's a 'maybe later.' "

"You're beautiful," he said to her.

"No, I'm not."

"It's not even worth arguing about. You are."

He kissed her. He kissed her neck. He kissed her chest. He kissed her arm.

"Another sunny morning," he said.

"Another sunny morning."

"I think the lid's been taken off," he said.

"Which lid is that?"

"The lid to my happiness."

"Do you think so?"

"I feel it. It's wonderful. I didn't think it could happen, but it's happened."

She caressed his face. "You see. I told you."

"You did," he said.

"What will you do?"

He grinned at her, and the grinning said that right now he didn't know or care. He gazed out the window, still holding her. With his arms around her he felt unconquerable, and the world was a good place.

"We can stay here as long as you want," she said. "We don't ever have to go back. We can, if you want to."

"You do believe me," he said.

"I believe you."

"Look at you."

"Can't we go crabbing tomorrow?" she said, moving against him.

"I've created a monster."

She laughed. "You have."

"We don't have to go crabbing today. We can lie around all day. I'll read from Birds of the East Coast."

"No, you won't," she said, capturing him with her leg.

"Okay, I won't."

"Kiss me."

"Again?" he cupped an ear.

"Kiss me."

"Once more?"

"Kiss me."

"All right," he said, and he did.

She had gone grocery shopping and was putting things away when she heard him come up the porch steps. By the sound she knew he had hurried up the steps. She was standing with a gallon of milk in her hand when he walked in, using an upturned shovel like a walking stick. His face was red and sweaty, and he had a damp, dirty circle on either shoulder from wiping his face.

"You're back," he said.

"I just got in," she said, and put the milk in the refrigerator. She eyed him suspiciously.

"What?"

"You're acting strange."

"I am?"

"Stranger than normal."

"Really."

"What's with the shovel?"

"Look," he said, and thrust out his arm. She took the shovel just below the head.

"What am I looking at?"

"What do you think of it?"

"I think," she said, turning it around to examine both sides, "it's in bad shape."

"It does have a little wear," he admitted, passing his finger over the sharp edge which waved in and out, but then came to a rounded point. "Well, what do you expect; do

154

you like it?"

"I love it," she said, and suddenly cradled the shovel and kissed it.

"Come on," he said.

"I'll keep it with me wherever I go!"

He took it back. "Fine," he said and walked away from her.

She put the rest of the groceries away. She found him sitting on the edge of the bed, his boots untied but still on, examining the shovel. She sat down on the bed beside him, without saying anything, watching him. She looked at the shovel. Perhaps she had missed something.

"It really is a nice shovel," he said to her.

"I can see that."

"Look at the handle," he said, leaning the shovel toward her. "See the grain. Feel how smooth it is."

"Wow," she said enthusiastically, rubbing her hand up and down the shaft. "It is smooth."

"He gave it to me."

"Who gave it to you?"

"The coal miner."

She shook her head.

"The coal miner who lived in the marsh. He and his wife lived there. An Irish couple. A tall, tough guy. You know, the *coal miner.*"

"I don't remember," she said. "Maybe you did tell me about him."

"Oh, yeah, a great guy."

"He just gave you his shovel?"

"He did," he said with a nod. "He came back to give it to

me."

"That's strange. Why would he do that? Did you ask for it?"

"He said he used it all those years in the mine, and it never broke. He used it in his garden. He used it to fill in around his house where the dog scratched holes. Did I ask him for it? Why would I ask a guy for his one and only shovel—especially a coal miner? Heck no, I didn't ask him for it."

"Then why did he give it to you?"

"He said he wanted to give it to me. He said he liked me, and wanted to give me something before they left. He said nobody ever wanted to be a coal miner, but when you were one you were proud to be doing something so difficult. He said this shovel enabled him to be something, even though he wanted to be something else. He said only a few people are what they intend to be, and everybody else breaks their backs trying to get there, or uses what they can to find another way. He said this shovel would get me there, but it was up to me to find out how."

She leaned back on the bed, kicking her feet, watching him. "So what are you going to do with it?"

"What am I going to do with it? What am I going to do with it? What else can you do with a shovel; I'm going to start digging."

XVI

A streak. Well, a smudge anyway; winter has a way of blurring the best of good intentions—our two runners are no exceptions. Up the long, pitted cement sidewalk, across the humped bridge noisily discarding its coat of ice and cinders on the tracks below, onward toward Goodwill Park and eager, leashed dogs.

"What a day, eh?" runner number one wheezes to runner number two.

"Unbelievable," two coughs back.

"The sun shines, the birds sing, winter is nearly defeated, and Jerry Wrigdd is in custody."

"Let's see how he likes iron bars and cold soup."

"That'll be the least of his worries for a pretty boy like him."

"Hee—hee—hee."

"Ha—ha—ha."

"He'll be singing a different tune all right. Two octaves higher."

"Ha—ha—ha."

"Ho—ho—ho."

"You hear where they found him?" wheezes number one.

"Yeah, on the coast."

"In some dumpy small town in North Carolina. He and Flower Child were shacked up in some shack, carrying on as if nobody was ever going to come knocking."

"Did you hear what they were up to?"

"You mean when the cops swarmed in?"

"Yeah."

"No, what?"

Runner two stops, short of breath. He coughs, then laughs, then nearly chokes, his face turning a nice Macintosh crimson. "They, they, they were digging a hole."

"Digging a hole?"

"Digging a hole, that's right. As sure as I stand here, that's what they were doing."

"A hole. In the sand?"

"A hole in the sand."

"What for?"

"They don't know."

"What kind of hole? There are all kinds of holes."

"A big one."

"How big?"

"Big enough for both of them to stand in with only their heads above ground."

They fell silent. Runner two because he was amused and

158

thinking, and runner one because he secretly admired Wrigdd, and because he was worried. They rumbled on a little farther. This time it was one who stopped.

"Tell me," he said, "what did they do when the cops found them?"

"Well, you know, that's sort of funny. Apparently ol' Wrigdd just raised up his hands like this and says something like, 'You're here.' And the girl—wouldn't you think she'd have been bawling or pleading? But no. She gets herself out of the hole, looks back down into it and starts laughing her head off. Man. What a kook."

"That's what she did?"

"You think I'm lying? 'Course that's what she did."

"Did they ask them what they were doing?"

"I don't think so. They just found them in the hole."

"He's sane, you know," runner one said.

"Sane? Aw. . ."

"Sane," he repeated. "They've already done a psychological evaluation on him. All the nuts and bolts are there. Sane as you and me."

"He's crazy, everybody can see that."

"No, he's not. And I'll tell you something else. He's not a druggie either. What do you think about that?"

"I already told you what I think. I think what everybody thinks—that he's a two-headed ass."

"I don't know."

"You don't know?"

"That's right, I don't know."

Runner two shook his head, then wiped the ditch of sweat trapped between the fold of his neck and chin. "Hey, one more thing. There's been movement."

"What?"

"On the land. I was driving by this morning and saw some trucks pulling in."

"What kind of trucks?"

"Big trucks."

"Cut it out with the big stuff. What kind of trucks?"

"Big yellow and dirty ones. Seriously. All kinds. All big, and all yellow, and all dirty. Even saw a few dirty construction guys with big yellow hard hats walking around."

"I'll be damned."

"Yeah, that's what I thought. He's not dealing, so I don't know what the hell's going on."

"Uh-oh," runner one said, putting his hand to his mouth.

"What?"

"Oh shit," he said, and fell against a brick wall.

"What?"

"Oh Jesus."

XVII

Billboards. Curious how you don't notice them until something truly unique is pasted up there. In mid-April, truly unique billboards began appearing all around Cowopolis.

Possibly the first person to view one of these billboards was a man by the name of Lester Scrump. After seeing his two little ones to bed, doing up the few saucers and cups left over from evening tea, and taking out the garbage, he thought he might sit beside his lovely young thing of a wife for a much-deserved evening treat. For this he donned his beige boxer shorts (the ones with the fish on them), one of his cleanest T-shirts, and a blast of Old Spice smack dab between his budding breasts. A quick brush, an even quicker rinse with mouthwash, and he was off to woo the Missus. To his utter surprise and disappointment, she was having none of it. It was her T.V. night.

161

"But, honey," Scrump whimpered, "every night is your T.V night."

"Shhhh," scolded the young Mrs. Scrump.

"But, baby," grovelled Scrump.

"Shush," came back the reply, "can't you see I'm trying to watch?"

"But—"

"Cut it *out*," Mrs. Scrump warned, and lightly poked him with a ready elbow.

Several more attempts of varying strategies—even one in which the school of fish leaped across her ivory thighs, pinned themselves against her fair skin, and began a vigorous foray upstream—got him nowhere. He retired to his study, feeling lonely and rejected.

Scrump woke a few hours later, slumped over his computer. Without going into unnecessary and sordid detail, let the record show that the fish had travelled far downstream, and on the computer screen in exquisite color and detail was the image of a (presumably) eighteen-year-old amateur contortionist, lacking clothes and demureness. It's difficult to say whether this image, or the rain beating against the window, startled him, but Scrump lurched backward and fell with a crash to the carpet. Quickly, he moved to normalize things, and in less than a minute the fish were again swimming merrily about his waist, the computer was off, and the appropriate hygiene was administered to desk and keyboard. He reached to turn off the desk lamp when something caught his eye. It glowed through the window, distorted, blurred from the rain.

"What's this?" he said to himself, peering out the

window. Moving his head, he viewed the glowing jumble of words from every angle, yet could not make them out. "Honey?" he called out, as he went to open the window. "Honey?"

The lovely young Mrs. Scrump entered the room. "What the hell are you doing?" she said from soft, sweet lips.

"Come here, come here," Scrump urged.

"You're going to wake the children. I was asleep, you know."

"Take a look," he said, pushing her to the window.

"It's cold," she complained.

"I know, hon, it'll just take a minute." He pointed her toward the billboard, though such careful orientation was hardly necessary.

Where only that morning there stood a vacant, vine-covered expanse of flaking colors, there now was a sheet of white, upon which the following yellow words were written, illuminated from below by bright lights:

Brendan O'Malley didn't mine coal
for the likes of you.

The Missus yawned, turned and said, "Who in God's name is Brendan O'Malley?"

"You're asking me?" Scrump blurted out.

"What's that supposed to mean: *Brendan O'Malley didn't mine coal for the likes of you?* I mean, what kind of a stupid ad is that?"

Scrump reread the words several more times to himself. "I think it's brilliant," he said finally. "We just don't understand it."

"Brilliant, huh?"

"Naturally. Most vague things are brilliant. That's why they're vague."

Mrs. Scrump looked at her husband as though he were a garden slug. "Why don't you stay up and think about it, Les," she said.

"You know I don't like it when you call me that," Scrump reminded her.

"I'm going to bed. Thanks for waking me."

"I'll be there in a minute," Scrump smiled, patting her on the fanny as she walked by him.

"You take as long as you need," she said, suddenly fleet of foot. "I know how curious you are. Gosh, I'm tired. . ."

Similar scenes occurred throughout the city. One group of boys on the near east side went out after school to shoot pigeons which sat on the ledge above the headless Marlboro Man. But when they arrived, the headless Marlboro Man was gone. Justin Chapwick, leader of the gang, tossed his bag of 5-10-5 fertilizer on the ground, then sat on it. The others, who were also lugging bags of fertilizer pilfered from their fathers' garages, followed Justin's lead.

"Hey, what's that?" one of the disciples cried out, spitting out a piece of grass he'd been chewing, and then pushing back and forth between the gap in his two front teeth.

"Hey, what, are you blind?" said Justin, who would have punched the boy in the arm if he'd been in reach.

Marco Polio

They stared at the new billboard:

Thomas Jefferson is mad.

"Any a you guys know who Thomas Jefferson is?" Justin asked, looking around at his followers.

"Thomas Jefferson?" a bright but unfortunately less than tactful boy sneered. "You don't know who Thomas Jefferson was? You're kidding. Ha—ha—ha. Wait till I tell my mom. Ha—ha—ha. . ."

In two seconds Justin Chapwick was sitting on the boy's chest, playing patty cake with his face.

"Okay, smart ass," Justin said, pinning the boy's hands above his head. "You gonna tell me who he is? And you better not laugh, or I'll fill you with fertilizer and blow you to smithereens."

"Okay," the boy squealed, trying not to cry. "Just don't hit me!"

"And you better not tell your parents either."

"I won't! I won't! Thomas Jefferson was our third president. He wrote The Declaration of Independence. Sorry, I thought everybody knew."

"Maybe every nerd like *you*." Chapwick sat his bag of fertilizer on the boy. He looked up at the billboard again. "If you're so smart, then what does that mean?"

"Beats me," the boy gasped. "Hey. When are you gonna take this off?"

"Any a you guys heard a this Jefferson guy?" Chapwick

asked, moving a pointed finger around the gang. Each boy reluctantly, modestly, admitted that they'd heard a thing or two about him. "Yeah? Well then tell me, how come that sign says he's mad if he's dead?"

The question required serious thought. They all sat on their bags of fertilizer, except for the first boy who still lay squashed beneath Chapwick's bag, and gave it their full attention.

Across town, beside the river, another billboard was drawing some attention. Lilly Prawn was lying in her sun bed when she was rudely distracted from her transcendental, medically prescribed therapy, by the sound of nothing. You would think that the sound of nothing is exactly what you would want during your thirty-minute medically prescribed session of melanoma and meditation; but when you're paying two men twenty-five dollars an hour to paint four bedrooms, two halls, a bath, and a library, that silence might as well be nails across a chalkboard. Lilly, after a full five-minute gaping hole in the normal, reassuring melody of manual labor, could stand it no more. Wrapping a towel around her cooked body, she went out to investigate.

"What's the matter?" she asked accusingly. The two Puerto Ricans looked at her blankly. "Why. . . aren't. . . you. . . work. . . ing?" she said to them, moving her hand in a ridiculous imitation of painting. She frowned, pointing to the idle rollers and pan.

"What is the problem?" the older brother replied.

"I asked, why. . . aren't. . . you. . . work. . . ing?"

"We work, yes," he nodded, grinning. "Twenty-five dollar an hour. Ten year experience in San Juan."

"Yes, I know," Lilly slapped the back of one hand into the palm of the other, "that's what I'm paying you. But you no work—comprendo? You stand a here and I hear no sound—slap-slap-slap—of the brush—comprendo?" The two men looked at each other. They didn't know what to say.

"Use your brain, save a nation," the older one said.

"What is this? I never see before."

"What did he say?" Lilly said, addressing the younger one, who stepped back shaking his head, pointing in deference to his bilingual brother.

"We see sign out there," the older one said.

"Out where?"

He turned, opened the French doors, and pointed:

Use your brain,
save a nation.

"Use your brain, save a nation," he repeated. "Eh?"

"Yes, I can see that," Lilly said.

"What is this meaning?"

"What is *the* meaning, and I don't know."

"Use your brain, save the nation. Es funny, no?"

"Very strange," Lilly said.

"Es strange, yes, I think so too."

So it went. Each morning brought with it new bill-boards, unlike any people had ever seen. You couldn't go a mile down Fifth Avenue, or two blocks on High Street, or sit anywhere downtown for that matter, without having one of those yellow messages staring down at you. A Sunday morning stroll for coffee and doughnuts became an ordeal, as you looked up and read the sign which you had read many times already and knew by heart; you looked anyway, you stared at it while bumping into lampposts and mailboxes and others staring the same as you, then placed your order inside the shop for a dozen glazed, three jelly, and one chocolate macadamia.

"Did you say a dozen glazed?" Bertie would say with a look of surprise.

"That's right," says you. A dozen, just like every Sunday.

"Plus three jelly, and a chocolate mac?" she'd ask, lifting her head above the glass counter as her tongs delicately snatched up the glistening goodies and aligned them neatly in a box.

"Right on the money," says you.

"Greed is not a virtue," came a voice. You tried to ignore it. "Greed is not a virtue," it came again. "You see that one?" Then, knowing now that the voice had directed its sonar at *you*, you found yourself caught in that quickly widening gap between thumbing your nose at common etiquette, and being drawn into The Conversation.

"What's that?" you'd say, longing for the days when waiting for your box to be filled was spent ogling the ones-not-chosen.

"The newest one," the voice said, followed by a brief squeak from a swivel seat, "up on Locust. Greed is not a virtue."

"Oh. Is that right?"

"What do you think of that: Greed is not a virtue?"

"What do I think? Hmm. I'm not choosy, Bertie. Any twelve will do."

"Have you seen it?"

"No," you lied.

"Yeah, it's right around the corner, above the laundromat. So. . ."

"What did this one say again?"

"Greed is not a virtue."

"Really. They seem to be getting stranger and stranger."

"Strange? What makes it so strange?" the voice deepened.

"Different. That's what I meant, I guess."

"You think greed *is* a virtue? Is that what you're saying?"

"Forget the chocolate mac, Bertie. Whatever you have there is fine."

"I think whoever is putting those things up there is right on the money. Better than seeing that other crap up there."

"True."

"So you think it's all pretty strange? Hey," and here you heard the swivel sound again and the voice doing a 180. "Harry. This guy thinks they're stupid. The signs, I mean. The guy in the fruity shorts."

"That guy?"

"Yeah, that's him."

"Figures," Harry said.

"Bertie?"

"Guess he'd rather see the big M's, or some lady in a

velvet dress, stretched out real provocative, there for all of humanity to lust after."

. "Guess he would."

"Yeah, well, what do you expect."

And all you were after was a dozen glazed, three jelly, and one chocolate macadamia.

The question of the day, of course, was who was behind it all? Although the billboards seemed to have nothing to do with the stadium, the immediate conclusion was that they came from the hemorrhoid of the year, Jerry Wrigdd. But there was a problem with this conclusion: Jerry Wrigdd said he had nothing to do with them. The question was rephrased many times and on many different occasions (it was suspected Wrigdd was pulling a Willy), to include any knowledge whatsoever of the billboards. Wrigdd answered by saying he wished he were responsible for them, but he had no knowledge of their origin.

An interesting phenomenon occurred. There were those, still the vast majority, who believed Wrigdd was lying. But there emerged an opposing view, those who believed Wrigdd was telling the truth, that the billboards originated from another source. Their argument was as follows: Although some of the billboards were ambiguous, many if taken at face value, were quite clear. And not only were they clear, but their messages had value. Therefore, Jerry Wrigdd could not be the one behind them, for everyone knew and agreed what a wretch he was. You found people who had been staunch Wrigdd-haters shifting their views, defending not his character, but his lack of involvement. This evolved, through a dangerous marriage of shoddy argument and haste, into a gradual defense of *him*. As the rift widened, and some of the attention moved away from Wrigdd to each other, the question remained: who was putting up the billboards?

The billboards weren't finished going up when heavy activity began at the stadium site. First the site was scraped level. The extra dirt was not made into a ramp, as is usually the case, but was hauled off in dump trucks. Then came the surveyors with their instruments, and sticks with their little nylon flags. They stayed only briefly, and when they left there was a perfect circle of small sticks outlining where the stadium should be. Crowds gathered around the site. Optimism ran rampant. The question was put to Usurper, who denied any ongoing negotiations with the incarcerated Wrigdd. Those trucks, he said, were not his. If the people wanted answers, they'd better go to the source. Wrigdd was asked. Unlike when pressed about the billboards, he did not deny involvement. He sat for most of the interview in quiet reserve, his silence broken only with his standard reply, "It should be obvious what's going on."

Well! Everyone knows what, "It should be obvious what's going on" means. Even a two-year-old in diapers knows it can be translated into, "Of course, you idiot. Who else do you think could be behind it? But because of legal intricacies beyond the scope of human imagination, our good friend, Mr. Usurper, is forced to deny, deny, deny. Celebrate, good citizens. The war is over!"

As the semi's with their oversized loads of steel girders, wooden planks, corrugated tin, and portable outhouses flowed like oxygen-starved blood from outside the city walls toward the epicenter, people followed them, tossing flowers, hands held high in the now ubiquitous V for victory. Businesswomen planted themselves unabashedly in the laps of grizzled old drivers, offering kisses freely. Confetti fell from windows, horns blew not in anger or impatience at the slow-moving trucks, but in celebration. Children climbed aboard like ants, and even the most overprotective mothers couldn't stand in the way of this once in a lifetime chance to ride aboard Liberation! At the gates, crowds swelled. Venders set up permanent residence, inflating the price of a hot dog from $2.00 to $3.50, that for a soda from $1.00 to $2.00, and a slice of cheese on your burger from 25 cents to 75. But nobody seemed to mind. In fact, people were in such an intoxicated state of brother-hood, that the little styrofoam cups designated for tips and normally used as miniature trash receptacles, overflowed with green, nickel, and copper tokens of appreciation. The trucks were sent through the gates as restorers of humanity.

Up went the scaffolding. People brought lawn chairs and blankets, and they stayed whole days watching the pro-gress. Boys rode over after school to sit on bikes and cling to the chain-linked fence with their fingers and mouths, and imagined the glory they would soon see taking place on their new field of dreams. In three weeks the scaffolding was complete. It stood a marvel of engineering itself, a full nine stories high. At sunset the thousands of X's sparkled so brightly you could not look at them.

I suppose it was when the canopy went up that people became concerned. The canopy covered the whole thing, scaffolding included, and when propped up in the middle looked like a gigantic circus tent. No one had ever heard of putting such a canopy over a stadium in progress. It was argued that the canopy would keep out the sun and rain, and thus was an innovation, a victory for the workingman. But there were other concerns. Take, for example, that plans for the new stadium called for an irregular egg shape, not a round one. Why would the scaffolding be round, if the stadium was to be an egg? Maybe they changed the design. Maybe that's what some of the hush-hush between Usurper and Wrigdd was all about. Everyone loved the egg design. Maybe they had to change it and were afraid people wouldn't like it. Then there was the machinery. Where were the big cranes? Oh, there were two smaller ones that were recently brought in, but not the enormous ones you usually see for a building of this magnitude. Even more disturbing was the absence of cement and brick. Everyone knows that when you construct a stadium these days, you need a seemingly endless supply of both materials; but there were no cement trucks, and no pallets of brick being brought in.

When digging for the foundation began, there was a sigh of relief. Some of the more rabid fans took it upon themselves to organize a ribbon-cutting ceremony. Neither the mayor nor Usurper showed. Usurper had stopped receiving calls concerning the stadium, while the mayor was rarely seen in public. Word from city hall was that he had a bad case of the flu. This failed to dampen the spirits of the true believers, however, and the ceremony was the major event of spring.

Down at the old bar, Wrigdd's old booth became a shrine. The booth became so popular it had to be managed by a reservation system, booked two weeks in advance. The meal and drinks were predetermined and included in the price of the booth: a basket of crackers, one soft pretzel with mustard, and pints of Burning River.

"You're a bunch of idiots," someone said, one evening, to a group of young professionals standing in a semi-circle around the booth. No one heard the man. "You're a bunch of fucking lunatics," the man said, and meandered off to the bathroom. The man passed the booth again on his way back. "Assholes," he muttered to himself. Someone heard him, a girl, and when she told her friend, a bodybuilder and growth hormone addict with a shaved head, what the man said, he stepped forward and confronted him.

"Who did you call an asshole?" the growth hormone addict said.

"All of you," the man replied with slow but lucid eyes.

"Hey, man, what's your fucking problem?"

"Stupid fucks like you, that's my problem," the man said.

Normally by now the addict would have been a whirl of moving fists. But in sizing the man up he noticed that although he was older, he was wide and meaty, and more than that his eyes had no fear in them whatsoever. His hair stood up in stiff curls. His jacket and hands were blotted with grease.

"What gives?" a less edgy, more humanly proportioned individual said, smiling. "We're just here enjoying ourselves."

"Tell me," the man said, addressing him, "have you seen any of the trucks lately?"

"Not in the last couple days, no."

"Not in the last couple days; in the past week?"

"In the past week, sure. I think I was there on Wednesday."

"What did you see?"

"On the trucks? I don't know. Steel girders. Equipment. And stuff."

The man moved his head up and down the boy's frame. "And to think, little twerps like you are running corporations. Well, friend, you know what I saw? Conveyor belts. That's right," he said, his voice in nearly a whisper, his eyes moving knowingly to each of them. "And the biggest, baddest drills I've ever seen."

"So what?" the addict, flexing his tattooed, crossed arms, said.

"So what? So *what*, did you say?" The man looked around at them, one by one. In their eyes he found innocence. Even less than that, he saw unconcerned ignorance. He was used to seeing it in the eyes of almost every person born from his own generation. But now, perhaps because he was drunk and tired and pissed off from working so much overtime recently, the vacuous eyes looking back at him flicked at the nerves of someone who had in his time struggled for something worthwhile, which now, to an entire generation, was a joke. "Christ," he said, rolling his eyes, shaking his head. He looked at them as if they were the most pitiful things he had ever seen. He walked away, talking to himself.

XVIII

Theo Usurper stood beneath a dripping umbrella just outside the fence to the construction site. It was early morning. Only a few men walking their dogs were about. Usurper motioned for one of the workers to come over.

"Hey, so, what's going on?" Usurper asked brightly to the man on the other side. He motioned for him to come closer, but the man stood where he was, about ten feet away. Usurper pushed his fingers through the holes in the chain links; his fingers flickered like moths. "What's that you're making?"

"I don't know," said the man.

"You don't know? What do you mean, you don't know?"

"You're Usurper, aren't you?" the man said with the dumb expression of someone having recognized celebrity.

"Yes, that's right."

"Thought I recognized you," the man said, grinning up coyly from a lowered head, stomping the dirt. "I thought that was you."

"It's me. Yup. So. If you don't know what it is you're working on, can I talk to the foreman?"

"Can you talk to the foreman? Oh, no, I don't think so. No, you can't talk to the foreman, Mr. Usurper."

"Why's that, son?"

"Oh, because. That would get me fired. They're paying me good money. I don't want to get fired."

"They'll fire you; *who* will fire you?"

"You know," the man grinned, stomping the dirt, "your buddy."

"My buddy? I have lots of buddies," Usurper smiled.

"Who do you think?" the man said looking at the dirt, still stomping it.

"Him?"

"The foreman won't talk to you. He don't want to get fired either."

"He hired you?"

"No, your buddy didn't hire me, a guy by the name of—"

"I realize he, personally, didn't hire you; but *he's* the one who brought those trucks and pieces of machinery in here?"

"Well, no, I believe a fellow by the name of—"

"Son," Usurper interrupted, moving his fingers through the holes in the fence. "Son, come closer. I can barely hear you. No need to worry."

The man checked behind him. He shuffled forward, his

head sunk into the collar of his work jacket.

"Son, you sure you can't tell me what's going on here?"

The man eyed the hundred dollar bill jutting like an extended finger through the fence. He checked behind him again, brushed his nose with his sleeve, then took the bill.

"All I know," the man said after taking the bill and then stepping back a few paces, "is we're digging a hole."

"A hole?"

"Yes, sir. That's all I know."

"You mean you're digging the hole for a foundation," Usurper said. "A foundation for what?"

"No," the man corrected. "A hole."

"I don't understand. You're sure of that?"

"Sure I'm sure, 'cause I was in the meeting when the foreman opened up the envelope."

"What envelope?"

"The envelope with the letter that said what we were here for."

"And the letter said you were to dig a hole?"

"That's right. Didn't say nothing about a foundation, or a building, or anything else. Only thing it covered was the hole. And that nobody was to say anything about it or they'd be shit-canned."

"Did the letter give you the dimensions of the hole?"

"Only the foreman knows the exact details. He's got the blueprints. It ain't my business to know what kind of hole I'm working on—know what I mean? Leave that to the higher-ups."

"Did the letter indicate how long it would take to dig this hole?"

"Well, we got a six month contract for starters," the man said. "I guess that's your answer. Six months."

"To dig a hole?" Usurper replied.

"I guess so. Ain't that something. Six months and all we're going to be doing is digging a hole. Ain't that something. Well, gotta get back now. Don't want to get shit-canned. Um, thanks. For the bill, I mean."

The man hurried back toward the tent and was lost again in the moving figures.

Denial is a powerful drug. For weeks the citizens of Cowopolis explained away what was becoming more apparent with each dump truck that emerged from the tent, bounced noisily past the gate, and crawled from the city to places unknown: there was no secret deal between Wrigdd and Usurper, and whatever it was they were doing at the stadium site, it had nothing to do with a new stadium. Slowly, people stopped coming to set up their lawn chairs and blankets. The vendors stayed for as long as it was profitable, but eventually went back to their old spots below office towers and near bus stops. The old denial, that there couldn't be anything *but* a new stadium being built, was replaced by a new one, that there was nothing going on whatsoever. The noise was incredible. It was so loud you could hear it, faintly, two miles outside the city limits. For those who lived within a mile of the site, the sound vibrated windows and influenced the volume on your T.V. It continued day and night, with little pause.

Lester Scrump rocked Megan in his arms as she wailed. "Don't cry, sweetie, don't cry. There, there," he said and rubbed her soft chin with his finger.

"Do you think we should take her to the doctor?" Mrs. Scrump said as she closed the door to little David's room, then pushed the towel into the crack at the bottom of the door. Thankfully, he was sleeping.

"What?" Scrump yelled.

"I said," Mrs. Scrump cupped her hand and yelled back into Scrump's ear, "maybe she should see the doctor!"

Scrump pulled back, shook his head. Mrs. Scrump waited for an explanation, but received none.

"Why not?" she yelled into his ear.

"What?"

"I said, why not!"

"Because," said Scrump, "she's probably just got an upset stomach. Gas maybe."

"What?"

"I said, she's just got gas! She'll be all right!"

"Grass? What do you mean, grass?"

"What?"

"I said, what do you mean, grass!"

"Did you say grass, or gas?"

"What?"

"Did you say grass, or gas!"

"Come on," Mrs. Scrump motioned, and led him to the fruit cellar in the basement. She pulled the chain, turning on the light, and shut the door. "You don't think we should take her to the doctor?" she said, rubbing Megan's forehead. "Shhhh," she said, trying to soothe her baby. "It's all right."

"Why?" said Scrump.

"Les, she won't stop crying."

"I know, but it's just gas. She had it last night too."

"Maybe it's not gas," said a worried Mrs. Scrump. "Maybe it's something else."

"Something else? Honey, I know you're concerned, but we're not made of money, you know. I just don't think we should go see the doctor when I can tell for myself what the problem is. Look at her face. See how she kicks her feet? See her body shake? That's gas."

Mrs. Scrump, unconvinced, took the baby. "It's all right," she said rocking her. "Mommy and daddy are here. Shhhh. . ."

"See," Scrump said. "Better already."

"Les," Mrs. Scrump said, "Shhhh, hush now. It's awight. It's awight. Yes. It's awight. Les, maybe we should move."

"Move? What are you talking about?"

"You know what I'm talking about."

"Honey," Scrump said.

"I just think it might be a good idea."

"We've been through this how many times?" Scrump said through his teeth, throwing his hands into the air.

"But *look* at her," cried Mrs. Scrump. "Our poor baby. If it's not her, it's Davey. And if it's not them, it's me. This is no way to live," she said.

Scrump held his wife. "Honey, don't cry."

"What's happening?"

"Nothing. Nothing's happening," said Scrump automatically. "Shhhh."

"Why are they doing this?"

"Nobody's doing anything," said Scrump.

"Somebody is."

"No one is."

"Then how is it happening?"

"It's not," Scrump said, kissing the top of her head, stroking her arm. "It just seems like it is."

Across town, beside the river, Lilly Prawn washed her forest green sport utility vehicle for the third time this week. Her street was only two streets away from Chesterfield Road. Chesterfield Road was one of the main arteries that the trucks took on their way out of town. The dust the trucks created smothered everything along Chesterfield. Two short blocks away at Lilly's, the air was heavy with it. She wore the rain suit she'd bought for the aborted trip to the rain forest, along with rubber gloves, goggles, and a breathing mask. She had pulled the vehicle underneath the trees.

"At it again?" came a voice from across the stone wall. Lilly raised her head. "It's me," the voice came again. Lilly turned to see her neighbor, John, standing on the other side of the wall, holding the supple branch of a crabapple away from his face.

"Oh. Hi, John," Lilly said, lifting her goggles and lowering her mask. "I thought I was hearing things."

John, a retired dentist, wore a surgical mask to fend off the dust, but now pulled it down around his neck so that he could talk. "How's she running?"

"Wonderful," said Lilly, removing her gloves and putting them on top of the wall. "I just love it," she said.

"Any trips in the works?" said Doc John, squinting.

"Nothing immediate," said Lilly, "although Donald frees up next month and we just might take a trip down to Hilton Head."

"Oh, lovely."

"How about you; isn't it about time for your cycling trip?"

"Next month," said Doc John.

"That's right, I always forget. A whole week, isn't it?"

"Yes. Three hundred and twenty-six miles this year."

"Three hundred miles," said Lilly in amazement. "John, I don't know how you do it. I wish I had the energy."

"Fifty miles a day is all," said Doc John.

"Fifty miles?"

"That's nothing. Believe me, Lil', you could do it no sweat."

"Oh, John," Lilly said, pushing up her goggles which kept falling down her forehead.

"Your hostas are doing nicely, I see," Doc John said admiringly.

"Aren't they wonderful!" Lilly exclaimed. "I'm so happy with them."

"I've never seen that kind."

"Yes, aren't they beautiful? I bought them at a nursery thirty miles north of here that specializes in hostas. Other than a few types of ornamental grasses, that's all they sell."

"They go well with your ferns, and the dark stone there."

"Thank you. It's been warm already this year. I'm afraid if I don't water them every day they won't make it."

"You're a born gardener, Lil'," said Doc John coughing,

"I'm sure they'll flourish." He lifted the blue surgical mask up around his chin and placed it over his mouth and nose. "Well," he said through the mask, "back to picking up these sticks. They're everywhere." He lifted the small bundle of sticks which were in his hand.

So it went. There you sat Sunday morning on your front steps, picking at the small pieces of crumbled cement, waiting for your son to use the bathroom. Next thing you knew you were walking down the street, holding his hand, off to get the doughnuts. Each time one of the trucks went by it coughed black smoke, its gate banged as it went over potholes, and it sprinkled gray dirt in the street which was then kicked higher into the air by cars. Your boy pulled his arm rapid-fire and the truck, with its tinted windows all around, honked.

"Don't," you say sternly to the boy, jerking his arm. You keep your eyes down, to the sidewalk, away from things that might spoil a Sunday morning walk with your son. When you arrive at the doughnut shop you let him open the door and then close it once you're inside. But he doesn't close it completely. As you're bent over looking into the glass display case you notice people are staring at you, and even more so, at the boy. Someone in the corner yells, "The door!" You immediately shut it, apologizing.

"Hey, Bertie," you say, and Bertie just looks at you as though both her motor and mental skills had been tampered with. Your son stands on his toes and pulls himself up so that his chin rests on the counter. The man sitting in the swivel seat beside him looks down unsmiling. "Don't do that, son," you say, and make him stand beside you.

Marco Polio

"What'll you have?" Bertie says, breaking the silence.

"A dozen glazed, two chocolate cream sticks, and two custard."

"A dozen glazed?" says Bertie, folding the flat cardboard into a box.

"Yes," you say smiling.

"Plus what?"

"Two chocolate cream sticks, and two of those custards there."

Bertie watches your son through the glass as she selects the dozen glazed, and it turns into a game of peek-a-boo. The man in the swivel chair watches them. He offers a finger like a worm on the edge of the counter, but the boy is too absorbed in the peek-a-boo game. Others in the shop who notice watch your boy, and they're happy for a time and forget the shadow that consumes their lives.

"How old is he?" an old man who you should know by name, but don't, asks.

"Three-and-a-half," says you.

The man says nothing, then says, "I remember when I was three-and-a-half. . ."

"Oh," says his wife, who sips coffee from her white cup, then chuckles, "you do not."

"Come here," the man says opening his hands. But your boy won't go. He lifts his eyebrows staring at the big, white-haired creature, shakes his head, then grabs your leg.

From one street over, there comes a sound. The laboring sound. The mystery sound. The sound of evil. It moves slowly, banging and grunting. The doughnut shop falls silent. Eyes are lifted, they move left, then right, to each

185

other, reassuringly. Smiles vanish except for your boy who is too young to know any better.

"Shhhh," you say to him, pulling his arm. "Quiet," you say, pulling it again. When you see that he isn't listening you pick him up, frown, and shake your head. You whisper in his ear that the game is now to be very, very quiet.

After the sound passes, you see that the old man has turned back around to stare past his wife out the front window, the man in the swivel chair drops a handful of change on the counter and then leaves in a rush, and Bertie is looking at you without expression of any kind, having already rung you up.

Digging continued beyond the predictions of even the most pessimistic men, and then beyond the adjusted predictions. People began whispering in the cataclysmic language known only to generations who have endured rare comets, or earthquakes, or pestilence, or genocide. It was estimated that The Hole had already reached half a mile. Rumors abounded. Some said he was boring beneath the city and one day soon it would fall into ruin. Some said he was going to put something down there, but what it could be they did not know. Some said they did know, that he was going to bury nuclear weapons beneath them all and set them to explode some time after his demise. Some said he was searching for gold, or diamonds, and this was further proof of his insanity. But no one asked him. The Hole was something incomprehensible. They carried on as the occupied, submissive people of the devil's army.

XIX

The days leading up to the trial passed quickly. She saw him each day for a half hour, usually in the early afternoon. They talked through the glass pane as though nothing were wrong. There was a calmness about them that prompted the guards to talk amongst themselves. It was eerie, they thought. Some of them pitied her, sure she had been lured into the trap of a madman. They seldom talked about the trial. The only time they did was in reference to some newspaper article she had brought in, and it was always for the purpose of laughter. She dressed prettily, usually in a skirt, with flowers pinned in her hair. Often he sat quietly and looked at her freckled face and burned her image in his mind. She brought him things to eat. She made him pies, baklava, cookies, and nut rolls. She shared them with the guards on her side, and he shared them with the guards on his. The guards eagerly accepted their offers, but secretly thought such generosity to be strange in the face of such a grim future together. It only added to their assertion that he was mad, and she was brainwashed. Of course, none of them knew about their nights.

It was an evening like all others, except for the heavy rain which fell steadily and powerfully outside. She sat in her kitchen watching the rain, moving crumbs of toast along the surface of the table with her finger, wondering about him, thinking back to the ocean, reliving their time together. She thought it strange how at the time one moment seemed to blur into the next, whether they were moments spent sitting in the chairs rocking together, or down at the dock watching the birds, or walking in the sand, or rowing in the boat, or making love; but now she could remember each moment distinctly and clearly, and she realized how short their time together really was. Even their conversations now crystallized, and she could remember some of them word for word. She hadn't taken their time together for granted. She knew then that it would probably be short, but had decided that you could either observe the time elapsing, or live it. She had chosen to live it. Now that the initial jolt of his incarceration was over and she was back at work in her daily routine, the brilliance of those weeks filled her with both contentment and emptiness. From moment to moment, she flickered between these two diametric emotions. The memories were so fresh and vivid, at times she felt she weren't remembering, but moving, experiencing. She could feel him near, his presence, his voice, his touch.

She closed her eyes. The memories passed through her,

and she fell into a strange, vague dream. When she opened her eyes she felt nauseous, fatigued, and it took some time for her eyes to focus. She concentrated on a spoon lying at the edge of the sink. For a while there were two spoons, and when she tried to look at just one of them it kept moving away, just beyond where her eyes focused, until she brought her eyes over to where the spoon actually was, and it started again. The two spoons eventually merged into one. When she stood up things were moving, as though parts of the room were molten. This made the few steps to the sink quite difficult. She latched onto the counter and gathered herself—she thought she might be drugged—and tried to remember if she had taken medicine or pills of any kind. She knew she hadn't. She felt sure she would vomit, and remained stooped over the sink, holding her stomach. Without looking she reached up and turned on the water, preparing for it, but the intensity passed. She was left with a warm, flushed sensation in her abdominal muscles, the way you feel after heavy exercise. From the cupboard she took a glass. She filled it with water, and still clutching herself with the other hand, drank it down.

She set the glass on the counter, and there in the window directly in front of her, she saw a face. She blinked, but the face did not go away. She closed her eyes for as long as she could bear before curiosity and fear forced them open again. The face hadn't moved. It floated in the window, neither close nor far away. Neither clear nor completely obscure, a face and nothing more, looking straight at her.

The face was not menacing, or frightening. It was strange, in the way that all new experiences are strange.

The face was that of an old man, the lines on his face cut deep demarcations between cheek, mouth, brow, nose, and eyes, and each of these features were like independent plots of wheat, or rye, or corn upon that face which served not as a readable history for a life lived long and varied, but as a product of it. It was not a flat or flabby face. The lines did not come as a result of too much drink, or stress, or too little of what life needs to thrive; the lines were as beautiful and necessary as each stroke of a painting by a true master. The face looked back at her with the directness and honesty found more in rural peoples than in cosmopolitan peoples. There was no false promise, but also no false motive. The face reflected that now rare quality of someone having understood life in its larger sense, by having understood it in all its small parts.

There was something familiar about the face. She was certain she had never seen it before, but she felt she knew it. The eyes reached across the short space, through the pane of glass, in a sort of longing, as though they had endured something and were still enduring it. The face whispered something to her. She could not hear it clearly. It whispered again, but she still could not hear the words. She called out to the face—and without thinking she threw up the window, stuck her head through the opening and desperately tried to reach it. It moved away from her to a point far beyond her reach, smaller now than it had been. And then it vanished.

She went to bed reluctantly that night. She lay facing the window, thinking of the face. She waited for its return, but there was only the rain falling outside, and nothing more.

Marco Polio

In the middle of the night she found herself on the floor. She thought she must be dreaming. She soon realized that she was sitting on her knees, her hands were raised above her, pressed against something. It was the wall. Everything was dark, she did not know if her eyes were open or closed. Her knees ached, as if she had been sitting on them for a long time. But the aching in her legs was secondary to another sensation that flowed throughout her body. This dominant sensation was pleasant, like a low vibration, or buzzing. It entered through her hands, and spread out within her. She lapsed back into sleep, or so she thought, for soon she was dreaming for certain—perhaps a dream within a dream—though there was nothing identifiable in it, only the strange, pleasant sensation.

Something pulled on her hand. Another hand. It closed around hers and then gently tugged. She felt herself moving, being lifted from the floor toward the wall, and then passing right on through. As she passed through the wall, the sensation increased. The vibrations reverberated within her. The hand was like a giant transformer, her body like some slumbering valley. Suddenly, she was awakened, as though she *had* been sleeping.

She felt him, moving through her, lighting forgotten or never-used filaments of her soul. She felt within her a new energy. Not for running, or working, or even thinking, but a capacity for acceptance. In this new capacity old fears washed away, solutions came easily, frustration dissipated. It was as though her lung capacity had been doubled, or tripled, so that with each breath she received double or triple the life sustaining force. Her consciousness rocketed skyward, then burst into a million points of light. She knew, in an instant, what was happening, and why. It came so easily that she could not comprehend her own former ignorance. It was as baffling to her as why moths fly willingly into flames. She saw the varying inherent ruts of mankind, they were as easy to discern as the flow of rivers from above. She understood—without judgement—the constructs of our kind. It was all there, laid out for her like a child's book.

The sensations changed. Suddenly a gush passed through her—exhilarating, swift—and she felt his presence. Now she was uncertain of her consciousness, for it seemed as though he was truly beside her, as though once again they were on her bed with the salt air breezing past, looking, caressing, moving. The feeling became less abstract, and she was able to see him, to feel his touches, to hear his whispers. He moved within her, she was lost in her ecstasy.

She woke in the morning feeling hot, fatigued, but refreshed. She remembered the night in minute detail. When she saw him that afternoon, she sat without saying a word for nearly the entire half hour, until the guard told them they had five minutes left.

"I had this dream," she said to him.

He looked at her, his eyes glimmering brightly, his mouth fixed, as though he had been waiting for her to begin.

"Was it a dream?" she asked.

"I don't know; what was it about?"

"Too many things."

"Tell me one of the things then."

"Well," she said, "there was a hand. It reached inside me. It did things to me. This morning I woke up and I'm not who I was yesterday." She paused, then said, "I'm like you."

"Tell me," he said leaning forward so that his head butted up against the glass, "how are you like me?"

"I see things now. I feel things. I used to think I saw, and felt, but now I know I saw nothing and felt nothing. Something has taken residence in me."

"Something you welcome?"

"I can't imagine it not being inside me. I can barely remember what it was like before."

"You're only talking about one day to the next."

"I know. But it might as well be one lifetime to the next. I'm as different from who I was yesterday, as I am from when I was a child. I feel as though I know, superficially, what lies beyond death. My soul is now mobile, where before it was attached to this body, limited to its movements, its inborn demands, its learned, repeated behaviors. I am able to pass through concrete walls, mobs, rote beliefs. They are like air for my wings—my soul is no longer confined by them, but is nourished by them, feeding off their falseness, gaining strength by the minute. All that was previously gravity weighing me down, is now thrust pushing me up.

"I now know what you were talking about all those times. I know because it is flowing through me. I see beauty beyond description, power beyond comprehension. I feel the id of generations taking me."

She unconsciously moved closer, a little frightened by

what she would say next. "I know who you are. You're not who I thought you were, not exactly. I had an image of you, a hope for who you were; but now I see you clearly. You are not the answer; the answers pass through you, they are accessible through you. You are a conduit through which others speak, and are heard; where hearts meet. I love you. Take these three words as deficient symbols of what my heart feels. I love you. I am yours."

He sat back in his chair, and for a moment he seemed slightly shaken. But then his expression changed, and he seemed pleased. He reached up and placed his hand flat against the glass. She understood, and placed hers opposite his.

From then on, each night was a beginning. Her days were not consumed with the anticipation of their half hour meeting across glass, but of the night when she would drift into half-consciousness, find herself kneeled on the floor before the wall, and move with him. Each time was like having another layer of compassion, empathy, humility, spread upon her heart. She came to love him more than she thought possible, and through her love for him the river flowed and gathered the pieces and made them into a whole.

XX

The trial began beneath a cloud of dust and smoke. Digging went on steadily, even as the weary crowds waited outside the courthouse, and then when it was time filed inside as though they themselves were jurors here to perform a duty. The newspaper and television crews were there, filming, and squawking, and pushing; but you could see the lack of enthusiasm in their pushy efforts. They were there to do a job, to cover a story, and most of them wished they had other stories to cover.

The defendant, Jeremy B. Wrigdd, was led into the chamber with the assistance of two men, one on each side, who held him under his arms and guided him between the rows of wide eyes. His hands and ankles were shackled, he shuffled his feet so that they made a sandy, scraping sound against the floor; the chain rattled dully link against link, disturbingly. Because the men held him beneath the arms, or perhaps because of his natural perverse nature, he held his arms out before him, hands at eye level, as though offering himself or something to those present. His movements were carefully watched and compared with the imagined persona that had been created over time by rumor and fear; his eyes revealed fanaticism, and quiet belligerence. Here was the lunatic, self-proclaimed time traveller, professional sports hater, mastermind of the eighth—and sole diabolical—wonder of the world. Rosaries were said. Many could not look directly at the demon.

His hands and ankles were unshackled. As the charges against him were read he appeared neither defiant, nor fearful, nor did he wear false courage. When asked how he pleaded, he answered that with all due respect he could not make a plea. He said that the trial itself would illuminate his guilt or innocence. He added that he was as anxious as anyone to hear the final verdict against him.

"You've been appointed a court attorney," said the judge. "However, you have indicated your desire to represent yourself."

"Yes, sir."

"It's not too late to change your mind."

"I appreciate it, judge, but that's the way I want it."

"Very well. Ladies, gentlemen, let's begin."

The prosecuting attorney, a short, over-eager man with a face like a decaying apple, stated his case. He thrust out his miniature chest, raised his squeaky voice, rolled up and down on his heels in self-assured neurosis. He sneered at the defendant, and it seemed sure hissing would soon follow. When he had finished his opening statement, he marched back to his desk crowded with books and laptops and adoring assistants, his face flushed. He sat down with all the aplomb of a first day substitute teacher.

The defendant stood up, and began making popping noises with his mouth.

"Mr. Wrigdd, are you all right?" a concerned judge asked.

"Just thinking, judge," answered the defendant.

He told the jurors he was sorry it had come to this, but that sometimes enlightenment is an uncomfortable, even painful process. He said he had no death wish, but that he was prepared to die for truth. This shouldn't be seen as foolhardy, or naive, or courageous; but merely the unstoppable impetus of one man. He said he would not force his beliefs on them. It was up to each and every individual to judge for himself whether his actions came from a delusional madman, or from one who understands what they cannot yet understand. Finally, he told them that the decision not to sign away his uncle's property for the building of a new stadium was the sanest, easiest decision he had ever made, and he hoped that during the course of this trial they would discover why.

The prosecutor brought forth one witness after another. He had a good, perceptive mind, but a bruised and caustic one. It became apparent that at some point in his life, probably in youth, he had been the object of ridicule and tormenting; his arguments bore the heavy wax of too much effort. He asked his questions, thanked his witnesses, then marched back to his seat. The judge would look down woefully at the defendant and ask if he would like to question the witness. The defendant invariably would shake his head no. The judge reminded him that although he could call these same witnesses later on, he ought to be cross-examining them now if he hoped to prove his innocence.

Jackie Tripp worked at the library downtown. He was called by the prosecution to testify on the third day.

"You work at the library on Mill Street," said the prosecutor, one foot on the witness stand, a thumb pushed full hilt into the top of his pants.

"Yeah," answered Jackie with fast-blinking eyes.

"What do you do there?"

"I re-shelve books."

"Is that the man you saw nearly every day for over a year," the prosecutor said, pointing to the defendant, "sitting in the same chair, his face buried in books?"

"Yeah," said Jackie timidly.

"You told me before, Jackie, that it was odd, the behavior of the defendant. What was odd about it?"

"I don't know," said Jackie blinking.

"You told me the defendant sat in the corner for hours at a time, alone, reading."

"Yeah," Jackie said perking up, as though his memory had been triggered. "That's right."

"It *is* a library after all. There's no crime against a man who wants to spend all day reading in a corner, is there? But the defendant drew your attention, Jackie. What was it that drew your attention?"

Jackie Tripp gazed around the room. Never in his life had there been so many eyes looking at him. "His crying," he said.

"His crying?" said the prosecutor, acting as if Jackie's response surprised him.

"You know, crying."

"How often would you notice the defendant crying, Jackie?"

"Some days more than others. Not every day."

"Would you say once a week? Twice a week?"

"About half the times I'd see him, he'd be crying."

"Well, Jackie," the prosecutor said in dramatic fashion, "that is a bit unusual, isn't it?"

"Yeah, I mean you get little kids that cry all the time, 'cause they're kids, you know. But you don't too often see grown adults crying like that."

"Agreed," the prosecutor said somberly. "Do you know why the defendant cried so often?"

"Not really," Jackie said.

"Did he ever confide in you or any of your co-workers as to what was causing his distress?"

"Nope."

"Jackie, did you ever see what books the defendant was reading?"

"Sure, 'cause you're not supposed to re-shelve the books yourself. That's my job."

"Did the defendant read one certain type of book, or did he read over a broad range of subjects?"

"He only read one kind."

"And what kind was that, Jackie?"

"History books."

"History books?"

"That's all he read. Every single day."

"Any particular kind of history? Military history; English history; ancient Greek or Roman history?"

"American history."

"*American* history?" said the prosecutor, tapping his lip. "I see." He gazed at the defendant puzzlingly. "Jackie, do you know of any other patron who sat crying in a corner reading American history books?"

"Huh-uh. Like I said, only little kids cry sometimes."

"Do you know of any patron who sat crying in any corner of your library, reading any kind of book?"

"No, sir."

"I see. All right, Jackie, that's all. No more questions, your honor."

For the first time since the trial began, the defendant stood up. He approached the witness with what can only be described as urgency.

"Jackie," he said, "who do you love more than anyone else in the world?"

"Is this a trick question or something?" Jackie snickered nervously, lifting his eyes to the judge.

"No, it's not a trick question," the defendant said, waiting for a reply.

"I don't know," Jackie said, rubbing his hands back and forth across his thighs. "My mom, I guess. My girlfriend's going to kill me."

"Your mom. All right. I'd like you to do something. Will you do something for me? You're not bound legally or in any other way to do it, but I'm asking you as a favor." Jackie nodded agreeably. "I want you to read a book.

You've got several copies at your library, it should be easy to find. The book is called *Bury My Heart At Wounded Knee*. Can you remember it? Before you start reading, Jackie, I want you to go through the book and cross out the Indian names, and write the word *Mom* above the names you crossed out. That's an easy thing to do, isn't it?"

"Sure, I guess so," Jackie shrugged.

"I want you to read that book, Jackie. I want you to read it with all those Indian names crossed out, and the word *Mom* written above them. And everywhere you see the names of Indian tribes or nations, I want you to cross them out and write the word *Americans*. So wherever you see the word *Sioux*, you'll cross it out and write *American*. Everywhere you see the word *Arapaho*, you'll cross it out and write *American*. Everywhere you see *Cheyenne*, cross it out and write *American*. And where you already see the word *American*, I want you to cross that out and write the word *Savage*. Read that book, Jackie, and then after you've read it, if this trial is still going on, I want to call you back up here and have you tell us what you thought about it. There are hundreds of books like it, with similar stories about similar people. That's just one book—a drop in the bucket. I'm just asking you to examine one drop out of that whole bucket full. Jackie," he said, "that's all I have for you." The defendant turned to the judge. "No more questions, your honor. Everything the witness said during the prosecution's questioning is true."

The next witness of note was the nurse at the hospital. She ascended the witness stand with short, deliberate steps. She would not look the prosecutor in the eyes, but fixed her gaze on the defendant, who looked back with reassurance and kindness.

"Miss Connolly, you've been a nurse for six years," the proseecutor said loudly and annoyingly, "is that right?"

"I have."

"You were on duty when the defendant was admitted to Riverside Hospital earlier this year."

"I was."

"Miss Connolly, would you do me the honor of address-ing *me* with your responses?" the prosecutor said. He moved over so that he stood between the defendant and the witness. "Miss Connolly?"

"Yes?"

"Miss Connolly."

"I'm listening."

"The defendant, he'd had a nervous breakdown. It was a bad one, wasn't it?"

"Are there good ones?"

"Will you please answer the question."

"He was pretty bad off."

"The defendant was bound for almost forty-eight hours."

"That's not unusual."

"He lay swearing, screaming at the top of his lungs."

"That's what a nervous breakdown is," the witness said.

"He could only be calmed by sedatives. Massive amounts of sedatives."

"Very much the norm for someone in his condition."

"Very much the norm, for *who*, Miss Connolly?"

"For those who can't accept it."

"Accept what?"

"Whatever it is that most of us accept, I guess."

"That would be reality," the prosecutor said sarcastically.

"That's the usual word for it."

"But isn't such a person, someone who denies what is real, what everyone else readily accepts; isn't such a person mentally flawed?"

"Yes, if the reality is worthy of acceptance," answered the witness. "But no, if the reality is not. Under those circumstances, I'd have to say that such a person is actually superior, in mental terms, to those who accept what should not be accepted. Do you view a man who sits calmly inside his burning house while it consumes him, to be mentally superior to one who rushes out like a lunatic?"

"We aren't talking about burning houses, Miss Connolly."

"Aren't we?"

The prosecutor was about to say something, but refrained. He shuffled a few steps away from the witness, head down, finger tapping his lip. Suddenly, he spun back around.

"Miss Connolly, what do you think of the defendant's so-called ability to travel through time?"

"I wish I could do it," the witness said.

"You wish you could do it; yes. I'll bet everyone in this room wishes he could as well. But do you *believe* the defendant?"

"It doesn't matter. It doesn't matter to me if he is or was insane, it doesn't matter if he's perfectly healthy. The fact is, his actions indicate a clarity of vision the likes of which I, personally, have never seen. If he were to have a fantasy of time travel—and I'm not saying it *is* a fantasy—it's no worse than the fantasies you all believe in to help you get through the day."

"You're suggesting the defendant is an atheist?"

"I didn't say anything of the kind. I'm saying that the human mind, at times, seems to need fantasies to avoid self-destruction. I accept this. It's just that your fantasy and mine may not be the same."

"Then *you're* an atheist," the prosecutor said.

"I didn't say that either. I said I believe in one thing; it doesn't mean I don't believe in another thing too."

"Back to the defendant, if you please," the prosecutor said, dissatisfied with the way the questioning was going. "Let's assume for a moment he *is* delusional. Let's assume he really can't travel through time. Let's assume it's all in his head. I know, we're really stretching it here," the prosecutor said lifting a facetious eye to the gallery. "The defendant may have been at one time an upstanding citizen, sensitive to issues few take the time to consider. But over time, perhaps because he saw that he could not alter things the way he wanted to, he became frustrated, embittered, and withdrew from social activities. He met a woman. A beautiful woman. A special woman. For a while, she relieved his loneliness. She shifted his focus from negative thoughts. He was happy. But then, sadly, she passed away. That was it—the uncorking of a sinister mind. All the negativity came rushing back in like a tidal wave. Some-thing happened inside him. No longer could he be content with isolation and loneliness; he had to impose his misery on others. He is presented with an opportunity—his uncle's land and fortunes. It's the perfect match. He goes to work. Calculating, vindictive; a rage against humanity smoldering like hot embers inside. He brings the community—and seeks to bring our entire society—to the verge of collapse.

"It's not that difficult to understand, ladies and gentlemen," the prosecutor said, by now addressing the jury and not the witness. "It's fairly clean-cut, this tragedy."

"Mr. Dickson," the prosecutor said softly, hands hanging limply and uselessly at his sides, the air in his lungs dropped down to his abdomen now and not squeezed into his tiny chest, eyes tired-looking; all in a concerted effort to be the common man.

"Just Dickson, no Mr."

"You work for Theo Usurper. In what capacity?"

"Info gatherer. You know, like how we were hunters and gatherers. Me, I'm still one of them. I'm a gatherer."

"I see," the prosecutor said with an ache to his face. "Your associate—"

"His name is Cheeks."

"Cheeks."

"You don't want to know why."

"Mr. Dickson—"

"Dickson, plain Dickson I told you."

"You and Cheeks paid a visit to the workplace of Miss Mary Green last summer, is that right?"

"We sure did."

"Why were you sent there?"

205

"To gather the info. That's what I do."

"Right. Tell us, would you, what Mary Green had to say about the defendant."

"Everything?" Dickson said in frightful recoil. The horror of high school oral reports came rushing back to him. "Word for word?"

"Paraphrase, if you like."

"Locksmith."

"She said the defendant, in so many words, was a locksmith."

"Not in so many words—in those exact words."

"Did she say why?"

"Sure she did. She said he had more than two eyes— eyes that could see just about everything; a heart that passed through boundaries; arms that reached around the world. She was speaking metaphorically, you see."

"Tell me, Dickson, how would you characterize Miss Green's relationship with the defendant?"

"Spooky. Kind of eerie-like."

"Spooky?"

"Spooky, like when somebody gets all misty and soft-spoken about somebody. I think that's spooky."

"Miss Green, in your opinion, seemed drawn to the defendant."

"I guess you could say that."

"Why do you think that was?"

"You're asking the wrong guy," Dickson said, and then put both big paws on the railing. "'Cause she's as nutty as he is, I guess."

"Mr. Dickson," came a reproachful voice from above.

"Sorry, judge."

"Dickson?" the prosecutor said, still waiting for an answer.

"Why does anybody fall for a guy like that; he's a man with a plan. Some girls go for the man-with-the-plan type."

"And what plan did the defendant have?"

"Oh, I don't know," Dickson grinned, holding himself as he chuckled. He slapped his knee. "I don't know. Rat-tat-tat-tat. Gee, I don't know. Rat-tat-tat-tat."

"The Hole."

"Looks like a plan to me."

"Dickson, what do you think the defendant's plan is, or was? Why do you think he's digging that Hole?"

"Nobody can see into a mind like that," Dickson said.

"What do you think he's doing over there?"

"Look, I don't know exactly. But I know what I see. I see that guy taking this city down the toilet. I see him digging a damn hole where our stadium was supposed to be. I see him laughing. I see a madman. Pure evil. Years ago he would've been lynched—lynched and people would have been thankful for it." His voice became sarcastic. "But you can't *do* that these days. The man deserves a *trial*, they say. That's the *law*. Hell, it's a joke. Everybody here knows it's a joke. Where the hell did law and order go in this country—that's what I'd like to know? Me and Cheeks and everybody down at the Raw Oyster, we can't figure it out. Nobody can figure it out."

Mary Green was called to the stand. The prosecutor, having no nails left to chew, put his hands in his pockets and rattled his change.

"Miss Green."

"Mr. Prosecutor."

"You're a 'friend' of the defendant."

"I am."

"The questions I have for you relate to this mystery thing or purpose the defendant claims he had for the proposed stadium site. Can you tell the jury what you know about it."

"I know it had nothing to do with football," the witness said.

"Yes, I think we've established that. What was it going to be then?"

"I really don't know."

"You don't know?" the prosecutor said, showing real surprise.

"He never told me."

"Miss Green, you're under oath."

"Mr. Prosecutor, the defendant never told me."

"He never told you, and you never asked?"

"I never asked."

"I find that amazing," the prosecutor said laughing through his nose. "Weren't you curious?"

"A little."

"But you didn't ask."

"I didn't ask."

"I must say, you're an unusual lady! I imagine most people wouldn't have had such control over their curiosity."

"Call it faith," Miss Green said. "Faith in the flesh and

blood of a great man."

"Blind faith, most would say."

"Faith by its very nature is blind. But my eyes are wide open to the target of my faith. It's something real, here and now, that I have witnessed with my own two eyes, and digested with my own mind; not something someone told me third hand, or that I read, or that was interpreted for me. A very informed faith, I would say."

"That could be a problem, if your mind weren't working properly," the prosecutor said.

"Then one person might be led astray. Not a civilization."

"Miss Green," the prosecutor said hastily, "suppose for a moment that you don't know what Mr. Wrigdd had in mind for the property. How about taking a shot at it now; what do you think the defendant wanted to build?"

"Why, so you can laugh at us?"

"Miss Green, no one is going to laugh at you."

"Not that I care."

"I promise."

"It's just that the country is full of comedians—why do you need me?"

"Please?"

The witness looked at the prosecutor, and felt sorry for him.

"I can't be sure," she said, "but I think he was going to build some sort of center."

"A center? A center for doing what?"

"A healing center. Something that as far as I know has never been built by human hands."

"A Betty Ford Clinic?"

"Something like that."

"Any idea who the patients might be?"

"A sick generation."

"Which generation?"

"Our generation."

"Yours, or mine?"

"This whole generation."

"What's the illness?"

"I don't know that it can be put into one word, or even several. But, Mr. Prosecutor, by asking the question you show symptoms."

The prosecutor was amused. "I must see a doctor when I have time. So. Mr. Wrigdd wishes to save us all from our—shall I say contagious?—"

"Very—"

"Diseases. Miss Green, if you *could* put it into words, this disease you speak of, what would you call it?"

"I don't know," she said. "I don't know what causes cultural entropy."

"Ah," cried out the prosecutor, wagging his finger, "a doomsdayer then."

"Not in the least."

"A modern Nostradamus?"

"Don't be ridiculous."

"A simple whiner?"

"To those who've called for the lowering of the bar, maybe."

"How do you cure such a widespread bug—a flood?"

"I told you, I'm just guessing. Maybe it can't be done.

But if I know Jerry, he was going to try."

"I've got it!" the prosecutor said snapping his fingers. "Mind control."

She laughed. "That's a tough cartel to break into."

The prosecutor, who had been halfway sitting on the railing swinging his foot, jumped off. He stared out the window. He surveyed what he could see of the city; its grayness, its film of dust which hung like smog above the smaller buildings and rimmed the taller ones, its people with their downtrodden faces. He turned his head so that his ear pointed out the window, and listened.

"What is that?" he whispered.

"Are you asking me?" Mary Green said.

"I'm asking you."

"It sounds like drilling."

"A center for the ill?"

She turned her own head and listened.

"Tell us, Miss Green, what it is."

"You know," she said, "I've heard it before, though I'm not sure where or when, or even if it wasn't just a dream I had. But it has the distinct, irritable drone of hope."

The prosecutor built his case upon repetitive, often illogical arguments. Without objections from the defense, he was free to do so with gross abuses to his profession, and open disdain for common ethics. So audacious was he, that several times the judge interceded on the defense's behalf, at which the prosecutor would grin coyly with embarrassment, and apologize.

For days the prosecutor called no witnesses, but went

from one soliloquy to another. You have to give him credit. His face may have resembled the rotting apple, his arguments were weak and unimaginative, but the man possessed oratory memory like a skilled politician. The jury found it hard to stay awake, let alone alert. But then there would come a thunderous boom—the prosecutor's tiny fist upon the table or railing—accompanied by words like, *traitor*, *vile*, *unforgivable*, and the jury would toss back their heads with eyes wide and mouths agape, and sometimes the mottled little head—or worse yet, the coffee breath—would be bearing down on them, only inches away. His weapons were not logic and proof, but fatigue and time.

The prosecutor called Destiny to the stand. Destiny was asked many of the same questions the prosecutor had already substantiated, such as how the defendant responded when asked why he wouldn't sell the property, what he intended to use the land for, and what sort of demeanor he'd displayed during the hearing. Destiny answered, respectively, "He thought the stadium was a dumb idea," "He wouldn't say," and "Slightly nervous impudence."

"You asked the defendant something else," the prosecutor said, snickering uncontrollably, grinning like a salamander. "You asked the defendant if he liked being an American. Mr. Destiny, how did the defendant respond to this question?" As if the judge had declared free cake and ice cream for everyone, both jury and gallery perked up.

"He said, I think his words were something along the lines of, 'I don't know. I don't know what that means.'"

The prosecutor brought forth one of his yellow pads. His

eyes sparkled as though he had just captured a new butterfly for his collection. "I can tell you, Mr. Destiny, exactly
what the defendant said. I have it right here. I'll read it to
you." The prosecutor, having waited for this moment for
days, strode to the center of the room and took the lapel of
his jacket in his hand, the way George Washington, or
Benjamin Franklin, or Alexander Hamilton must have
done, cleared his throat, raised his chin, and began to orate.

"The defendant's answer, when asked if he was proud to
be an American was, word for word, the following: 'I don't
know. I'm not sure what that means. It's not like asking
someone if he's proud to be Indian, or Jewish, or Chinese,
or Italian. If I were Italian let's say, and you were to ask me
if I was proud to be Italian, I could say yes—look at our
beautiful architecture which has influenced the world, look
at our art, look at our poets, look at our law systems, look at
our people with their beautiful olive skin and dark hair and
passionate hearts, their love of life and love of love. It's
much easier to answer, for in Italy, as in most other coun-
tries, nationality and race are more closely tied. Sometimes
they are nearly indistinguishable. But not here. The whole
point of this country is the separation of race from nationality. Religion from nationality. All other sub-groups from
nationality. Like no country in history, we are continually
being created by the influx of very different peoples, we are
a patchwork, a quilt. The question then becomes are you
proud of this quilt. Or more pointedly, are you proud of
how this quilt was made and how it is now held together.
That's not an easy thing to answer, unless you're blindly or
fanatically nationalistic. Am I proud of how this quilt was

made? I would have to say no. But how many nations, ancient or modern, are forged from cooperation among its different peoples, mutual prosperity, fairness? I can think of none offhand. Am I proud of how this quilt is now held together? More than proud, I'm happy and feel fortunate to live where individual freedom is so highly regarded, where real opportunity does exist, where the law protects religious, political, and cultural differences. And yet, there are millions of people throughout the world who have less external freedoms than we do, have far less prosperity, have little opportunities, who live better lives, are more content, are freer internally. I'm a man, not a symbol. I am proud if I belong to truth, beauty, fairness, moderation, intelligence. I am ashamed if I do not. Regardless of how you label it, regardless of its color, regardless of its traditions or institutions, regardless of its number of followers, regardless of its flag. Your question is meaningless outside a specific context. To be an American means to live at once on the wings of a dove, perhaps as few civilizations have lived. But also, precisely because there exists this vast potential, to live with sorrow, shame, and puzzlement at our collective ignorance when so many fail to reach those lofty heights.' "

The prosecutor, more pleased with himself than usual, stood staring at the jury, rolling back and forth on his heels. The elusive butterfly was held before them, pinned and mounted. "There you have it," he said. "In the defendant's own words." He dismissed the witness and strode back to his desk where he took short, noisy slurps from a glass of ice water, and blotted his forehead with a towel.

Destiny walked slowly from his seat between the prosecution and defense, and there he paused. He lifted his eyes from the floor, and looked around the room. For an instant it seemed as though he wanted to say something, but he remained silent, and walked out of the chamber.

The previous evening Jerry Wrigdd was lying in his cell when he was told he had a visitor. It was well past visiting hours. In fact, it was nearly time for lights out when he was taken to a room he had never been in before. The room was not secured. It was adorned with three naugahyde chairs and a table. When he entered the room the guard escorting him left and closed the door, and the man who was already sitting there stood up. It was Destiny. He didn't recognize him until he spoke and heard the soothing voice, somewhat weaker than he remembered, but unmistakable. Destiny had pulled up his goggles and tugged down his bandanna, which protected his pitted, cherub face.

He smiled appreciatively. "Thank you," he said. "So you've agreed to see me. Thank you very much. Sit down," he offered. They sat down in the big-armed chairs. On the table was a plate of meats and cheeses sliced into little wedges, and crackers. Destiny took a toothpick and began spearing cheese wedges. "Dig in," he urged, "they're for you."

"I'm not used to late night snacks," said Wrigdd.

"Sure. Ask any doctor and he'll tell you it's a bad thing," said Destiny. He rubbed his palms together over the floor and pushed the plate away. He chewed his final bite of cheese, swallowed it, licked his lips, then wiped his mouth with the back of his hand. "How are they treating you?" he asked.

"Like a criminal."

"You getting enough to eat?"

"I'm getting enough to eat."

"You've not been mistreated?"

"In *here*? In here I've been treated the way you'd expect to be treated."

There was concern on Destiny's face. But this superficial concern soon became dominated and then expunged by an obvious expression of deep thought.

"Did you want something?" the prisoner asked.

"What?"

"Why did you want to see me?"

"This is off the record, Jerry—you understand that? Anything said here this evening doesn't leave the room. We never met tonight." Destiny moved forward in his seat, and draped his forearms over his knees. His cherub face upon closer inspection was not so cherub-like anymore, but had grown thin. Gray dust clung to his skin like paint, where the skin had been left unprotected. His eyes were lethargic, as was his breathing. "I have a confession," he said. "Do you want to hear it?"

Wrigdd lifted his hands. "I'm listening," he said.

"For weeks now I've been wandering around the city," Destiny began, "like this, like others. We wander around moving our feet, searching for nothing I can put a finger on, it consumes time yet requires little thought. You might think it's thought itself we're after, but that's ridiculous; how can you think in a city like this, how can you do anything but wander around. There's the dust, the noise, the congestion from the trucks with their mystery drivers. A month ago only some of our streets were affected. Look at me. Look at what a walk through town does to you. The entire city is trapped, it lies in a haze. Women and children stay indoors, it's only the men who wander the streets to escape the questions with no answers, the crying with no chance of being soothed. I don't know about the others, I can't speak for them, but when I finally find my way back home I stand in the shower scrubbing my body of the dust, but it doesn't scrub clean. I've got open sores on my arms where I scrub and can't get it off. But then the very next day I'm wandering the streets again, I don't know why, I can't help it, there's no purpose in it. I stop and look for the sun, but the sun isn't there. It's behind the sometimes gray, sometimes yellow dust that falls from the trucks or floats in clouds from the. . . from *it*; the clouds remain over the city, even storms don't carry them off. This is how I live, this is how many of us live; but I think you know that. It's been your doing. I've thought of taking the family away from here, but this is our home, this is where we live, things surely will get better. I tell myself those things as I lie in bed."

Destiny paused, his eyes moved wildly. "I've been having dreams. I *think* they're dreams. I don't really know. It's usually the same, with only small variations. Here it is: The wanderers, we're all together. We're not free to move independently of each other, we're chained together at the ankles. Being chained together isn't too bad, the shackles don't hurt or cause wounds; nevertheless, we're chained to one another. We emerge from a great forest to a broad plain. We've brought tools, food, medicine. Our families are not yet with us. We've come to build a new village, here on the plain. Leading us are foremen. Some of these foremen brandish whips, and they use them on some of the wanderers. Some carry no whips, they are kind and shrewd and keep their own workers away from the foremen with whips. Everyone works hard. Whether you are motivated by the whip, or by trust, you exert yourself all day long so that by evening you collapse on a bench or in the grass or even while waiting in line for dinner. There is a leader who directs the foremen, but he is never seen. The wanderers doubt the leader's motives and abilities, and even his existence. They wonder how he can effectively direct the construction of the city from such a distance, and sure enough there are signs of his neglect, even incompetence, when footers are dug in the wrong places, or inadequate latrines are installed which pollute the water supply, or insufficient numbers of men are dedicated to working the surrounding fields which nearly starves the group. But construction continues, not necessarily smoothly, but steadily.

"You must understand. I'm describing this to you as if it definitely were a dream, which may be so. But while I am there it lasts a lifetime, I am there living these things, not merely observing them. They are as real as this meeting of ours. . . It takes many years, and many men die because of overwork, malnutrition, being whipped too often, or from mental illness. The village still has a long way to go, but the living quarters are completed, as well as some of the basic requirements for a community, such as a simple hospital, library, gymnasium, market. The women and children come. Children are bound to their mothers by long elastic cords which somehow do not tangle with one another." Destiny stopped, as though he was lost in his story. Soon it was clear that he was not lost, but frightened. He continued: "One day some of us were picnicking near the fields and silos. We had grain enough for two years—so successful had our farmers been. Someone suggested we burn down one of the silos for fun. I didn't understand. I thought the man was joking. 'What do you mean?' I said to him. 'That's insane. Why do you want to burn down what amounts to the collective work of all our men for two years, and more importantly represents our future? Are you feeling well?' But without responding the man produced a huge hammer and spike, and before long he and some of the others had freed themselves from the human chain. A group of women took scissors and severed their cords and flew with the men. Their children ran in haphazard circles, wailing. Before you knew it, the silo was burning. Flames flapped high into the sky and black smoke pumped into the air. I was dazed. The rest of us took our families back into the village and there, to our surprise, we found people dancing in the streets. There were bonfires everywhere. People danced and sang around the bonfires. The chains had disappeared entirely, the cords had all been severed. There was celebration like I have never seen before.

"It then began in earnest. They took torches and set fire to the village. They burned everything. The very village they built with their own sweat, the village which had cost countless lives, the village which housed libraries, and schools, and temples, and businesses, and art—all was burned in a single day.

"Jerry," Destiny whispered, seizing his wrist. "Who willingly destroys his own civilization? Oh, God," he cried, hitting his head with his fist. "It was the most horrible thing I've ever seen. We wandered for days among the charred remains of the village, past other homeless families now hungry and desperate. Finally, we went outside the village where we might find apples, or berries, or even grass to eat. It's the same as wandering through the dust and noise and congestion here; at times I'm lost and can't distinguish dream from reality.

"You're probably wondering why I'm telling you this," he said. "I can see it on your face. Or is that a smirk because you know all this already, because *you're* the orchestrator of this hell! No," he said, "forgive me. . . I'm wandering around *this* city, some days ago, when I bump into a man. I apologize, then continue on. But something compels me to stop and look back. When I do the man is still standing there watching me. He's old, very old, but surprisingly quick for an old man—you'll see what I mean in a minute. I approach him. He's got dark, leathery skin, alert eyes, large hands. When he turns his head left or right I can see a scarred neck, deeply furrowed, and then I realize I know this man! When we were outside the burned village wandering, looking for food and shelter, he took us in. He fed us, sheltered us. Why, it was the old farmer! He moves away from me. You would think I could easily catch him, but suddenly he's forty yards down the street. By the time I get to where he's standing, he's another forty yards away.

This goes on for the entire evening until the sun begins to set and we're on the edge of the city near the river. The old man is now on the other side, he's not mocking me, he looks back at me sadly. Then, he's gone. . . he just vanishes.

"I'm back in the city wandering around," Destiny goes on, "and there comes a voice, faintly, from somewhere. Is it from around the corner? A bus? From inside a building? Or, is it inside my own head? It grows stronger, becomes clearer. Do you know what the voice is saying?" Here Destiny cackled hysterically to himself until tears formed in his eyes and streamed down the sides of his bleached face. "The voice says to me, 'Jerry Wrigdd. . . Jerry Wrigdd. . . Jerry Wrigdd is right.' I told you I had a confession. Does it sound like one?"

The prisoner understood. He reached out his hand and shook Destiny's arm in reassurance.

"I had to come here. I had to tell you. I don't know what to say. I don't know what it means, or how I feel, or what is real and what is me going crazy; but I had to get it out. You're not the devil, are you? You're the furthest thing from it. Oh, what have we done? The misery. . ." he sobbed. "You've no hope. You're doomed. The next on The List!"

"Doomed?" Wrigdd said with a look of surprise. "No, friend. Not doomed. Freed."

When Usurper approached the witness stand the prosecutor, out of habit, went to shake his hand, but then shrewdly turned the gaffe into a retrieval of sleeve from jacket. He thanked him for coming. He apologized for the ordeal he had suffered during the past year, and promised to be brief.

"Mr. Usurper, tell the court, what was your desire a year ago when you agreed to purchase the downtown property of Adam Selowt?"

The witness, demure, fumbling with eyes cast in wounded magnanimity answered, "Why, I wanted to build a new stadium. A stadium for the people of Cowopolis."

"You wanted to build a new stadium for *who*?" the prosecutor said gently, as though he were dealing with someone fragile.

"The people, the fans. The old stadium was outdated. It needed too much improvement to make renovation worthwhile. The fans supported the Bovines for the better part of fifty years. I wanted to build a stadium everyone could be proud of."

"So it was the *people* you had in mind when you proposed the idea of a new stadium to the Cowopolis voters."

"That's right."

"Yet, you hinted that you would move the Bovines if Issue 1 weren't passed?"

"Without a new stadium the Bovines could not stay competitive. We were losing money. I wanted to light a fire beneath the city, which I think I did. The Bovines were forced to leave for Denver not because we didn't get a new stadium. The Bovines left because there was no stadium in which to play. The old stadium was sold, and already being demolished. We had no choice."

"You had no choice. But you did have a choice before. . ."

"Yes," the witness nodded, "but that was taken away by the defendant."

"The defendant, yes. You met with the defendant about the matter."

"Only once."

"That was last year when he was charged with, among other things, disturbing the peace and inciting a riot. Tell us about your meeting with him."

"I thought I could reason with him. I said to him, 'Look, I'm a reasonable man, you're a reasonable man. Why don't we forget the hard feelings and come to an agreement?' "

"Was the defendant receptive to that?"

"Not at all. He said he would, under no circumstances, sign the papers."

"Did you ask the defendant to reconsider?"

"Several times."

"And?"

"He wouldn't budge. He wouldn't discuss it."

"Did you explain what this would mean to the Bovines?"

"He already knew but yes, I explained it to him."

"And?"

"Nothing changed."

"Did you explain what this might mean not just to the Bovines, but the city?"

"I did."

"And?"

"No reply."

"I see. Mr. Usurper, did you explain what impact such an action—against the voice of the people, and here I refer specifically to Issue 1 in last year's election—what this action could mean for Football with a capital F?"

"I did."

"And?"

"This is getting repetitive, isn't it. The same thing. Nothing."

"Well then," said the prosecutor with desperation in his voice, "did you indicate to the defendant the implications to our nation, its people; that he might be better served to sever the supply of milk or bread or medicine or education if he wished us no harm?"

"I made it clear to him, the larger picture he was painting."

"Mr. Usurper," the prosecutor cried out, "did the defendant understand how many lives he would be injuring—even destroying—with his cruelty, that he was pulling the rug out from under his fellow man, that he was in essence playing God?"

The witness, eyes wandering, spoke softly. "I tried. I tried to tell him."

The prosecutor paused to collect his breath and wipe his forehead. "It's true that you attempted on many occasions to meet with the defendant, before and after this meeting?"

"I must have tried twenty, thirty times."

"The defendant would not budge, as you say. Wouldn't listen to reason. Over the months he grew belligerent toward your olive branches."

"He did."

"Was there a reason for his contempt? Had you done something to offend him?"

"No, but I believe the defendant sees our world differently than the rest of us. He plays by different rules. With his uncle's money there was no need for common decency toward me or anyone else. The will of the people had spoken, they wanted this stadium; but he viewed his own will to be greater."

The prosecutor caught hold of the cord and strummed it.

"The will of the people had spoken," he said, gravitating toward the jurors. "Ladies and gentlemen—did you hear that? The will of the people said 'yes' to this stadium. Not one man, not some outside force, but the people themselves. They looked ahead to their future and there they saw something better, something needed, something rare which has the ability to unite those from different backgrounds, different races, different religions. A house, if you will, in which the drama of every day life is played out by a very special breed of actor. Good versus evil. Weak against the strong. Rival versus rival. Love, conquest, rage, despair, hope—even war—is found between those sidelines. We watch these special players. Our lives are enriched by them. We gain an understanding of ourselves, our neighbors, and our enemies by watching. It is all there. The book of life."

The prosecutor took a drink with calculated slowness.

"One man decided to negate it. One man against the undeniable will of all others. One man, for selfish reasons he won't fully disclose, ripped apart this social contract." He turned to the jurors. "Treason, ladies and gentlemen. Treason."

225

XXI

The farewell party at the River Club was open to all. Donations were to go to some as yet unnamed organization, which had already begun campaigning to bring a new team to Cowopolis. Whether it was truly a new team from the next league expansion, or a pirated team from another city, it made no difference. A team was a team. Cowopolis would embrace it, nurture it, cherish it. The empty years without a team would be forgotten, after the appropriate period of mourning, like a deceased loved one. The future would be bright. There would be happy times again. It would be the beginning of a new era.

Cocktails were served an hour and a half before dinner. Most of the guests had never been to the Club before. They felt with their fingers the massive stone fireplace in the rotunda, or stood out on the deck where there was a breeze and looked down on the muddy river and imagined they were important and interesting and envied, so that when it was time for dinner and they were called in, they walked differently and talked differently and laughed with loud animation, and believed this was now going to be a life-style.

Dinner was your choice of chicken pilaf or baked white fish. Both were dry and cold. Some grumbled, but most were oblivious to it, and commented to those beside them how delicious and rare the food was. After dinner the acting mayor said a few words. The mayor himself had not been seen for some time. One Tuesday, weeks earlier, he didn't show up for work. No one noticed. His wife didn't think anything of it for three days and when she finally did, she thought she would use the opportunity to wallpaper the bedroom. Mayeye had been dead set against wallpaper in the bedroom. He said it would bring confusion to a weary mind preparing for sleep, and he was terrified it would contribute to his insomnia. The staff at his office carried on without much trouble. The first week they assumed he was spending time over at Usurper's. It was only when they called Usurper's office that they discovered he was truly missing. They waited another four days before calling his home. Mrs. Mayeye said she hadn't seen the good mayor in a while, but if they heard from him they should tell him to take his time, whatever he needed the time for. Staff members used the opportunity for long weekends, lunches, and phone conversations.

The acting mayor said some nice things about Usurper and all he had done over the years for the city. He was a transplant from Texas and received his information from a twenty-one-year-old intern who barely made it through business school. He kept it brief, which won him applause and admiration. Usurper, reluctantly, said a few words himself. He thanked the mayor, city council, and especially the people of Cowopolis who supported the Bovines faithfully through the years. He said he felt as though he were losing a family. He wished the city well. Theo Usurper was only a phone call away, he said. He would never forget them. With the possible exception of the bus boys clearing the tables, there wasn't a dry set of eyes in the place.

After dinner most of the guests flowed out to the deck for some air, to light up a cigarette or cigar, to gaze and be gazed at. Usurper stood with his back against the railing flanked by wives of ambitious men who were many years away from his stature. These women shifted their bodies from heel to heel like schoolgirls, sipping sweet drinks through straws, their earrings tinkling from laughter. For his part, Usurper was somewhat bored. He was particular about his admirers. He liked them tall, blond, flat-nosed, straight-toothed, white-skinned, smart, discreet, yet pliable to his wishes. The only woman reasonably fitting this description was on the other side of the deck. She was with someone, and for some strange reason was spending all her time by his side. Every attempt at eye contact had been ignored. She showed no interest in him, but hung wantonly on the shoulders of her date, as though she were drunk and ready.

"Excuse me," Usurper said in the middle of someone's sentence about nothing, and left the group with unaccustomed frustration, heading for the men's room. He stood at the urinal, bored with the evening. His mind drifted elsewhere. The gala was something of a nuisance. He was tired of living in two cities. The flying back and forth was wearing on him. At least his testimony was over. Finally he could move on, away from this dirty town. They could have their dirt and noise and congestion and trial, and he would be free of it. This last thought cheered him up. Yes, he would be free. Their burden would no longer be his burden. Their mess would be a foreign affair. He could forget the name *Wrigdd* and the yearlong detour in his life. In a few years it would be nothing more than a bump along memory's road. He rubbed his hands under the hot faucet. He looked at his face. He turned his head from side to side. In doing so he saw a flash of white, or thought he saw it, behind him. He turned, hands dripping on the floor.

"Who's there?"

He leaned to one side, enough to peer under the stalls. He was alone. He turned back around, pushed the large button of the hand dryer with his elbow, and rubbed his hands under the hot air. He made a mental note to himself to see a doctor. These illusions had been occurring more frequently. They were always the same. Quick white flashes, off to one side or behind him, never enough to distinguish a figure or object. He saw them here and in Denver; on the airplane, on the street, at home. At first they frightened him. But now that he knew they were illusions, he paid little attention to them.

He headed for the bar, obtained two gin and tonics, both for himself, and went to push open the door to the deck with his foot, when someone opened it for him. It was the woman. She held the door open as he stepped out, and then to his surprise and delight she did not move away. She stared into his eyes; what rich, deep eyes they were. They were plain eyes, yet somehow hypnotic in their directness and darkness.

She offered her hand. "Hello," she said. He balanced the two drinks in the cup of his left hand. He took her hand, squeezed it more than shook it. Her hand was rough. He instantly knew she used her hands for work, and she was not of his kind. He saw the lines around the corners of her eyes, the burned lips, freckled chest, all minimized by the dim light. It excited him. He was drawn to her foreign roughness as though she were a harlot from another world.

"Enjoying yourself?" he said.

"Oh, yes," she replied.

"Do you drink?" he offered her one of the gin and tonics.

"I do, but my friend is getting me one."

"Ah, sure. I wish I could say one of these was for a friend, but not true. I hate standing in lines."

"So does he," she said. "We've got a cooler in the truck. That's where he is now."

"What's your poison?"

"Beer," she laughed. "Just beer."

"Beer is good," he said.

"Would you like one?"

"Oh, no thanks," he said lifting the two glasses. "I've got these."

"Are you sure? It's just around the corner. We've got

plenty."

"What will your friend say when you show up with another man?"

"Oh, him," she shrugged. "He won't mind. Besides. You're not a man. You're the Usurper."

"Is that so?"

"Why sure."

He gazed at her then, openly, the test with no questions but many answers. She did not move or look away. She seemed to want his gaze. She seemed to want it now as much as she had rejected it before.

"You sure you don't want one?" she asked again. "I'll trade you," she said putting both hands over one of his glasses, allowing them to linger there, allowing him to feel the rough palms and long fingers and strength. "One of these for. . ."

"For what?" Usurper said, looking straight into her.

"For a beer," she said playfully, and began walking slowly.

"A beer. I do like beer very much. Sure, let's go for a beer. Sounds like a bargain. Is it?"

"A bargain?" She laughed, losing balance, falling momentarily against him. She said nothing.

When they got to the gate leading to the parking lot she stood waiting for him to open it, sucking on the little stir stick of her drink. He opened it, allowed her to walk through, watched her as she moved, and only went through himself when she stopped and turned, stirring the ice cubes with the little stick. The asphalt turned to gravel. She took his arm for support.

"It's not much farther," she said.

They were nearly at the end of the parking lot. There were only a few cars nearby. He saw no truck.

"Are you sure this is where you parked?" he asked her.

"I think so," she said, but her voice was not confident.

"But there's nothing out here," he said and stopped. "That's strange."

He looked in all directions. "What color is it?"

"Blue."

"What kind?"

"What kind?"

"You know, the make. Is it a Ford, a Chevy?"

"I'm not sure," she said.

He looked at her. "What do you mean, you're not sure?"

"I don't remember."

He dropped the drink. He took her roughly by the arm. "Look here," he said. "What are you trying to pull?" He shook her by the arm. "Out with it."

"That hurts!"

"You bet it hurts. Now, tell me what's going on."

"But there's nothing to tell," she said now without any false innocence, struggling to free herself.

Usurper struck her across the face. He struck her again. He took her by both arms and shook her. "*He* sent you, didn't he?"

"Let me go. I don't know what you're talking about."

He struck her several more times, then pulled her off into the pine grove. He threw her to the ground. She tried to crawl away, but he kicked her, then fell on top of her in a rage. He turned her face up and struck her repeatedly until she offered no more resistance. He pushed back her hair. Her face was red, not yet bruised.

"You were leading me to *him*," Usurper said through his teeth, "weren't you. Weren't you!"

"Help!" she tried to scream, but it only came out as a mumble.

"Where is he?"

"Oh. . . who? . . ."

"Him," he seethed, his eyes darting into the trees. "Tell me!"

"I don't know who. . . where are we. . . who? . . ."

"You were going to get me the way you got Mayeye. What did you do to him! Did you drown him? Shoot him? Strangle him?" Usurper put his hands to her neck. He closed them. Her face turned redder, her eyes bugged out. He squeezed with all his might. She clawed at his fingers and in a sudden burst of adrenaline beat at his face; but his hands did not move from her neck.

He watched as her face became the faces of others. He thought he was imagining it. He shook his head, momentarily relaxed his hold, but the faces kept changing, one after another, faces he did not know, faces similar only in their unfamiliar despair and misery; the faces of women, children, and worn out men, hungry or unlucky or ignorant. He watched as he squeezed the life out of them. He heard their cries for help, he saw their last gasps, choking, coughing, the eyes wild with impending death. The eyes! Though the sight shook him, he kept on pressing. Their desperation angered him. He felt as though they were forcing his hands. He closed tighter. He watched as their eyes rolled back, their mouths flew open, the air was purged from their lungs. He let go, and her head dropped limply to the mat of pine needles and leaves.

XXII

She slid the front page of the newspaper through the slot. He unfolded it and took his time reading it, glancing at the large photograph of Usurper, then back to the article, then to the photograph, then to the article. For the second day Usurper had gone to the police to report a murder. He told them where to find the body. He said there had been some sort of domestic dispute between a woman he'd met, and her husband. The husband became violent, knocking him unconscious. He strangled the woman to death. The police found no body. There was no sign of any struggle in the pine grove at the River Club. When Usurper persisted, he was told to go home and get some sleep. He said he didn't need any sleep. He was asked how much he'd had to drink that night, and when he fumbled for the right words the men in the station grinned and gave each other quick winks. He was politely escorted from the premises.

He finished reading the article. He looked up at Mary through the glass, moving his head so she was not in the glare. He could have looked at her and done nothing else for the whole visit.

"What do you think?" she said.

"I think I love you."

"About the article, silly."

"I think," he said, holding the paper in front of him, "I think I'm going to tape this article on my wall next to my April, May, and June centerfolds, above the tic marks, below the squashed roach, and. . . and it will be happy."

"Three centerfolds? You dirty boy."

"It's a dirty place."

"You don't seem worried," she said, concealing her own anxiety.

"Should I be?"

"I'm still not where you are," she said.

"Behind this wall?"

"No. Beyond the point of any fear."

"But you know, there *isn't* anything to fear."

"You're leaving. That's something."

"That's something to dread, but not fear."

"There's a difference?"

"There's a difference. The first one will leave an emptiness in your heart for a while. The second one can alter your perception of truth."

"Don't go," she said.

"There's no other way."

"I know. You know I know. I'm just scared, and dreading it."

"I've been a lucky man," he said. "To have loved, then lose that love, then find it again. I am the luckiest man that ever lived. Words can't express how I feel about you. Without you, I would have kept spinning. Without you I would have died. Without you none of this could have happened. I don't know why you've done these things for me, you have the gift of faith. You can see beauty and goodness where others see nothing at all. After last summer I didn't think life could be meaningful again. But you made me see that it could. I'm telling you because after tomorrow I might not be able to tell you."

"I love you, Jerry. It's that simple. It explains everything."

She ached to hold him, to feel his arms around her, to have his cheek against hers, to feel his heartbeat.

"I don't want you to die."

"That's not what's going to happen."

"You're going away. It's the same thing for me."

"It won't be. You'll see."

"Are you sure?"

"I am."

"I believe you, but, oh—why do you have to go! Now, when for the first time in my life I've found love."

"Mary," he said pressing his hands against the glass, "it's going to be all right, you'll see. After tomorrow the clouds will be lifted. It will be a new day for you, and Cowopolis. You'll barely know I'm gone."

"I'll die of loneliness and heartache," she said.

"No," he said. "You'll be happy. In some ways happier than you've ever been. I wish you could see it. Tomorrow is right before my eyes. It's in my hands, clear as a blue sky. You have to believe me."

That night she sat at the kitchen table after eating dinner and picked at what was left of her food, thinking about the man she loved, loved with every ounce of female blood in her body, loved without strings or plans for future remodeling, loved as you love a child, unconditionally and thankfully. She thought about what he had said. She wondered how not seeing him for the rest of her living days could be bearable. At times during her reflection, she regretted loving him. She weighed the pleasure and the pain, and came up with regret. But that was her heartache talking. Even now, as she sat perched on the cliff of loneliness, she would do it again. She would love him and be loved by him, and lose him. She would because though her life had not been bad before, she had been sleepwalking. She went along each day avoiding those things which caused her mental or physical duress, following the path to security and relative fulfillment. Her path had taken control of her life. She no longer followed it by choice, but was pulled along by it without consideration. She became like a tree in a forest, seeking a hole of light in the canopy. Her being was bent to reach that small piece of meaning and happiness. She waited for it, longed for it, dreamed about it, so that when she was given a small piece of it here or there, she felt if not satiated, validated. Like most, she believed in *Something*, a view of the way life should be, the world should be, the afterworld should be. This view evolved over time and was reached after much contemplation. It was a sensible view. A good view. But it was just like everyone else's *Something*; it limited her energies to consider other views. She had become, unwittingly, another Einstein in a world of Einstein's. She had become another lemming, because she believed *they* were the lemmings. She had become cynical, even prudish about sex and love, because her age and her loneliness dictated it. These shields against the barbs of the gauntlet were natural, and typical, and uniquely human. She was no different from anyone else. She had been like an abandoned car, rusting through the years.

She *had* been this way. But no more. He changed her. He changed her without trying to, and without her knowing it. Love will do that. It awakens the dead, heals the ill. It opens the senses, imagination, and possibilities. It can make brittle wood pliable again. It makes heroes out of cowards, and wise men out of fools. But he did more than that. He took less than he gave. He empowered her, so that she might escape the rigidity of her path. He illuminated the many truths, and squashed the idea of the false, single truth. He reconnected the lost cord to those who had come before, those who will come after, and those invisible souls she rubbed elbows with each day. Their blood, through him, flowed into her. It became clear: The human struggle toward happiness and fulfillment is sacred. It is perhaps the most sacred of all human endeavors—a basic right crossing boundaries of age, race, gender, wealth, religion, country, and generation. That which prohibits this struggle from maturing, from coming into fruition, is counter to human-ity, is anti-life, and is—if such a thing exists—the greatest of sins. Gradually, over the months, she had been arriving at this understanding, intuitively, abstractly. She now gave the abstraction form. Because she had combed it over and over in her mind, she could use it, as people will do, as a guideline, or formula. A new path. But because it was a path, formed from an abstraction in the human mind, she would not be bound to it. It would serve as her guide, not as her master. Always, the wisdom of perspective would be followed, before all else. For it is the human mind which creates a path, and the human mind must therefore manage it.

She sat for a while then remembering their time to-gether. She was moved to tears from the remembering. She knew that she would ache for him after tomorrow. She also knew it would be bearable. He lived inside of her. Not merely his spirit, in the figurative sense, but the life that made him who he was. She could not wholly distinguish between their two entities. His physical presence would vanish, but *he* would not vanish.

She slept, but then as she did each night, she found herself kneeling before the wall, the vibrations moving through her, the hand taking hers, pulling her through. She lay with him on his short bed, they did not leave the cell. She cried much of the time, and though he wanted to soothe her and give her comforting words, he cried too. He told her how precious she was. How he had spent the past few nights reflecting on their time together, and how it all went back to the same thing: her devotion and sacrifice for him. It humbled him, and made him feel unworthy of her. He told her he would miss sitting in the chairs rocking, glancing at her from beyond Birds of the East Coast; sitting on the dock down by the water watching the birds and fishes and sunsets and blowing sea grass; rowing in the boat to new streams, making love on the banks or in the boat; lying with his head in her lap as she sang lullabies to him and he drifted into blissful slumber; their days at the beach where there was room to run as far as they wished, where they swam naked to the sun, where they rolled in the sand and laughed with the sea gulls; the sound of her beating rugs with a broom, the clanging of dishes, the smell of Murphy's Soap; the sight of her emerging from a bath, or from the bed in morning, or lying asleep in the middle of the night with moon glow on her face, and especially the look of love she had in her eyes whenever she gazed at him. She said it had been like a dream, and he said it was a dream but a real one. They had been blessed, that was certain. Not many share love the way that they did. No, she said, but they should.

He kissed her. He would miss kissing her perhaps more than anything. All things became clear when he was kissing her.

XXIII

In the morning Lester Scrump woke feeling warm and content, the sun shining on his face. The lovely young Mrs. Scrump, surprisingly, was lying by his side, still in sweet slumber. He hesitated, but then reached out and draped his arm around her. His hand was not pushed away. He waited, but there his arm sat, resting heavy on her waist, skin against skin. He closed his eyes. With his eyes closed he blocked out everything but the sensation of warmth, and closeness, and serene breathing.

He slipped from bed and went downstairs to make coffee. He opened the kitchen door to let in the breeze, when he saw it. The billboard had changed. He shook his head, thinking he was imagining it, but there it was plain as could be, in simple yellow letters. He stared at the billboard, rereading it over and over. When the coffee was ready he poured himself a cup and sat down at the kitchen table. He struggled with what he had just seen. He sat without moving, until his wife came down.

"Honey, what's wrong?" she asked him.

Scrump lifted his arm and pointed. Mrs. Scrump looked up, and saw these words:

He was here.

She turned to her husband. "Who?"

Scrump trembled. He looked at his wife.

"Who was here?" Mrs. Scrump said.

Scrump's eyes began to tear.

"Lester?"

He hid his face in his hands.

All over the city, the billboards said the same thing. People awoke, opened their doors, and read the words.

When the guard went to see that the prisoner was up and getting ready, he found the cell empty. He dropped his keys. He unlocked the cell, his hands shaking, went in and tapped the bed covers, looked under the bed, and then ran down the hall blowing his whistle. There was a brief discussion with the head guard. He accompanied the head guard to the cell, who himself tapped the covers and looked under the bed. The warden was called at his home.

At the courthouse people had begun to file in. The judge was in his chamber when a page knocked on the door and was let in. The page handed him a small piece of paper.

The piece of paper read, "Defendant has escaped." The judge frowned, read the words again, and glanced up at the page who had a face with no answers. He dismissed the page. It was shortly after that when the phone rang.

"Hello," said the judge calmly.

"Judge Cranstin?"

"Yes?"

"This is Warden Bailey. It seems we have a problem."

"The defendant has escaped?"

"You got the message; it seems so. He's not in his cell. We've done a quick look around, there's no sign of him. We'll keep looking, naturally, but it doesn't look good. Funny thing is, there's no sign of the escape. His cell was still locked when the guard went to check on him. There's been no wire cut, nothing. Looks like somebody snuck him out, but that's impossible. Somehow he just disappeared. I don't know, judge, you might want to postpone things for a day. That's up to you though."

"I see," said the judge.

"It doesn't make any sense. He just disappeared. We've got the dogs out now trying to pick up his trail. We've also notified train stations, bus terminals, and airports in all adjoining states."

"I see."

"Of course, we've set up roadblocks at all the key routes around the county. Unless somebody dropped down out of the sky and snatched him up, we'll get him."

"Huh. . ."

"Judge?"

"Mm?"

"Oh. Thought I lost you. We'll get the little bastard. Don't worry about that."

"You'll call me when you find something?"

"Yes, sir, we sure will."

"All right. I guess that's that."

The judge hung up the phone. He sat stirring his coffee, thinking. He sipped the coffee, put the mug back on the desk, then folded his hands over his belly and twiddled his thumbs. He remembered the quiet composure of the defendant, who sat alone behind the big desk, watching and listening and saying very little. He remembered the witnesses and their testimonies. The testimonies seemed at the time to be bricks being laid around him, rising higher and higher, closing in on him. It had been sad to watch, especially with the defendant's reluctance to counter them. But as he thought about it, there came a different image in his mind. An image he did not conjure up—it just appeared. The testimonies were no longer bricks being layered around him, closing him in; they were wheelbarrows of cement being poured into shoes, and boots, and pockets. The shoes, and boots, and pockets belonged to the men who had previously been laying the brick. These men were being rowed out into a swift and wide river and were being dumped overboard. The judge sipped his coffee. He sat at his desk thinking, though his thinking was not getting him very far. His coffee turned cold.

"Well," he said to himself. "Okay then."

The jurors were told to go home and wait to be called back at any moment. As days turned into weeks, which turned into months, they were told to go back to their normal lives. The trial was suspended indefinitely.

Digging stopped. It took some time for people to notice, but by late afternoon goggles had been tossed into the air, coveralls were stripped off, and there was wholesale celebration. The trucks continued to flow, but only in one direction—out of the city. Their big beds were empty; tailgates banged in glorious staccato.

It would be tempting to say that things soon went back to the way they were, but that would be inaccurate. The Bovines were gone. That single fact implied vast lifestyle changes for the average Cowopolitan. The yearlong siege against the city, like any real threat to life and limb, left its mark. There was renewed appreciation for sunny days, clean streets, solitude, and most importantly for fellow citizens who in general stood by each other throughout the crisis. Then there was The Hole itself, that unmentionable cavity which could not be reversed. It sat there, near the edge of the river, ignored, a minor obstacle for pedestrians and cyclists and civic planners, but no longer the menace it once was.

Mary Green waited until one early January night, and then went, accompanied by her brother, to visit The Hole. The fence was still up. Nothing much had changed on the site except that the digging had stopped, and the men and trucks were gone. Her brother cut through the fence with a large pair of snips, and they stepped inside.

The ground was frozen. There were deep ruts and narrow ridges of hard earth from machines rolling over the previously malleable mud. Snow covered these ruts. It was impossible to predict when you would step into one. They proceeded with caution.

"We shouldn't be here," her brother said. He led her slowly with his arm out like a handrail.

"It won't take long," she told him.

"It's creepy here."

"We'll be in and out in ten minutes."

"Yeah, well, it's still creepy here. Mary," he said, "I don't get you. How you got hooked up with a guy like that, I'll never know."

"Is that what you think?"

"Is that what *I* think? No, that's what mom thinks, and dad thinks, and gram, and everybody in Cowopolis thinks. You're smarter than that," he said, turning to look admonishingly at her.

"A million people can't be wrong?" she said.

"It should make you wonder. We really shouldn't be here."

"I know. You said that."

"Nobody's been here since. . ."

"He disappeared?"

"*Shhhh.* Don't say that. No, since last summer."

"Where do you think he went?"

"*Doooon't.*"

"Well, you must have thought about it."

"No, I haven't."

"Really?"

"Come on, sis, don't. You're freaking me out."

"All right. But it's hard not to wonder."

"It's hard not to wonder why we're here, when nobody else is."

"I'm here because I loved him—"

"Don't. Don't even say that," he said shaking his head.

"Why not? It's true."

"I don't care if it's true. You didn't know any better."

"I'm here because I *did* love him, and you're here because you're my brother."

"Jesus, it's cold," he said. "Jesus."

The big canvas tent still stood intact. The bottom flapped bitterly with the sound of the cold. The tent filled suddenly, then the bottom lifted and the air came out like a giant breath.

"Look," he said and stopped, pulling on her arm. "I'm not going in there."

"I don't expect you to."

"I never said I'd go in."

"You can wait here," she told him.

"Okay. Right, I'll wait here," he said, coaxing her forward, stepping backward. "I'll keep a lookout."

She pulled back the canvas, which when not flapping hung stiffly, its creases frozen over. She felt her heart beating and turned toward her brother, but he had moved away from the tent to sit facing the city with its lights, shivering and talking to himself. She stepped inside and clicked on her flashlight.

She had never been to The Hole. No one had except those who had worked on it. She moved the beam of light up and down, searching for the edge, and when she found it she moved the light slowly all the way round. The size was something unexpected and it overwhelmed her. With short, cautious steps she inched closer, until she stood two feet from the edge. Warm air rose from below and bathed her face like summer wind. Each night since his disappearance, she remembered, and pondered, and believed, though she was not certain what, exactly, she expected from it. She closed her eyes and it all came back, it was as though they were together again with the sun on their faces and the sea breezes filling their lungs. She thought of him sitting on the dock, or in the sand, his face full of joy and freedom. Or coming in from a morning out in the marsh, giddy, his face darkened by the sun that he loved. She felt the warm air rising from The Hole and imagined they were flying together, like hawks floating higher and higher, rising always toward the sun. What it must be like, she thought, your world without useless complexities, only the breeze and your wings which were designed for breezes.

From beneath her coat she brought forth a large envelope containing copies of all his poems. For some time she sat holding the envelope, tears came, but she was not afraid. She took the poems from the envelope and let them fall, one by one, into the unseen depths of The Hole.

No one knows who the first person was, or when he came to lie around it, but within two years they were coming in large numbers. At first they came at night, secretly, sneaking in through the first slice cut by Mary Green's brother. Then they began to cut new slices all around the fence until it was shredded and could be passed through easily at any point. They came and lay with their heads toward The Hole, arms and legs extended, like butterflies, in concentric circles around it. During that first summer they dismantled the tent because it blocked the vast night sky with its innumerable stars. By mid-summer a few had begun coming in daylight. First only a few, but soon the others followed. The second winter came and the number of pilgrims did not dwindle, but increased. Those who came to lie near it included many former enemies of its builder. They came reluctantly, skeptically, some with the purpose of spitting into it, and many did just that. Those who walked past could not understand the people lying around The Hole. They laughed at them, ridiculed them, threw bottles at them. The travellers, as they called themselves, said that it possessed magical powers, and they were forever changed by it. They said that lying around it in quiet meditation was like sitting in a room with all the great thinkers, writers, leaders, and peacemakers, each pouring his life's wisdom through a tube into their minds and hearts. They said that people throughout the ages spoke to them, filling their souls with humility. They said The Hole was like a magnet, and once you had aligned yourself to it properly, you were forever bound to it, you were freed from the real chains, and you gained that which had eluded you all your life.